A Fa

A fascinating no
of Granada Telev
the Ashton family of Liverpool in the early
years of World War II.

A Family at War series

A Family at War
A Family at War: To the Turn of the Tide
A Family at War: Towards Victory

KATHLEEN POTTER

A Family at War

from the Granada Television series
created by John Finch

GRAFTON BOOKS
A Division of the Collins Publishing Group

LONDON GLASGOW
TORONTO SYDNEY AUCKLAND

Grafton Books
A Division of the Collins Publishing Group
8 Grafton Street, London W1X 3LA

Published by Grafton Books 1989

First published in Great Britain as a
Mayflower Original 1970

ISBN 0-586-20920-4

Printed and bound in Great Britain by
Collins, Glasgow

Set in Times

A Family at War

CHAPTER ONE

Margaret Ashton hurried down the road, walking briskly past the semi-detached Edwardian houses towards the one which was her home. This was one of the better areas of Liverpool. The houses were roomy and well built and the street was graced by a few trees.

This road was very familiar to Margaret. She had lived in it all her life. Her parents had come here when the houses were almost new, at a time when society had seemed settled and solid. Now, in 1938, the world was a very different place.

Today was Jean and Edwin Ashton's thirtieth wedding anniversary. Margaret, the eldest of their five children, was organising a small family party to celebrate the event. She was on her way home to make sure that everything would be ready by the time her parents arrived. Her father knew about the party, but it was meant to be a surprise for her mother. Edwin had promised to keep Jean out of the way until seven o'clock.

Margaret looked at her watch as she turned into her own front gate. It was already half past six. She hoped that her younger sister Freda had been getting on with the preparations while she was out.

The stained-glass panelled front door was on the latch. Margaret went into the hall and put the packet of serviettes that she had just bought down while she took off her coat. Freda came through from the kitchen.

Margaret grimaced at the tangles in her short dark hair and pushed it straight.

'Are we ready?' she asked Freda. 'Did you look at the stove for me? Has anybody come?'

Freda refused to be harassed by Margaret's sense of urgency. She was a happy-go-lucky kind of girl.

'It's only half past six,' she said. 'I looked at the stove. And Sheila's here—she's in the kitchen. She came on her own. She says David's following on later when he gets back from work.'

'Good.' Margaret mentally calculated who had yet to arrive. As well as herself and Freda and Philip who were at present at home and their married brother David and his wife, she had invited her widowed Uncle Sefton and his son Tony to the party. That, since the youngest Ashton, Robert, was away at Nautical School, made a total of nine people. They would need a chair bringing down from upstairs.

'Where's Philip?' she asked Freda.

Freda laughed. 'In the living-room,' she said, 'laying the table—man style.'

'I'll go and see how he's getting on.'

Philip was standing by the piano. He had the lid of the music stool open and was leafing through a pile of sheet music, looking for something to play. Philip, lately, had become adept at wasting time and usually Margaret tolerated it. She knew, as did all the family, that Philip was feeling rather unsettled. Now, however, she said: 'I thought you were laying the table.'

Philip waved a hand towards it. 'Done,' he said. 'Finished. A work of art.'

Margaret looked it over, checking on all the items that were set out.

'Do you call that table laid?' she said. 'What do we eat dessert with?'

Philip walked across the room to stand beside her. 'Mm,' he said. 'You're on to something there, aren't you?'

'Oh, come on,' said Margaret. 'Let's get a move on.' She liked organising. 'Freda, get the dessert spoons and for heaven's sake put a zip in it.'

Freda smiled her perky smile and pulled a face at Margaret. 'Hey,' she said, 'you're not at school now, Miss Ashton.'

Margaret clapped her hands to shoo Freda out. 'Allez-vous-en,' she said, teasing. This was exactly the kind of occasion that made Margaret happy. She loved to have all the family together. In spite of her brusque and sometimes rather distant manner Margaret was warm-hearted. To her, the family was very important, something that must always come first.

In this she was different from Philip. Philip, like his father, was politically aware. He owed allegiance to causes outside his home. A few months earlier he had left Oxford where he was studying modern languages and gone to Spain as an interpreter with the International Brigade.

Margaret would never understand why he had done it. At home, seeing the anxiety and distress of her mother, she had been sure that his idealism was misplaced. As far as she was concerned, Philip owed far more of a duty to his family than ever he did to some peasants in a foreign land.

She had been glad when Philip's venture had ended ingloriously. Four weeks ago he had been sent home for an appendix operation from which he was still convalescing. Margaret heartily hoped that that was the end of the matter and that when he was properly better Philip would go back to Oxford. She dreaded to contemplate what the effect on her mother would be if he went back again to Spain.

When her father got home Margaret was in the middle of rearranging the table. Edwin walked through the hall quietly. For a heavily built man he was surprisingly light on his feet.

Sheila heard the front door open. She peered out of the kitchen and saw him.

'Hello,' she said. 'Should you be here so soon?'

Edwin smiled at her and put a finger on his lips. He wanted to surprise Margaret. Sheila smiled back and nodded conspiratorially. She liked her father-in-law. In the nine years that she had been married to David, Edwin had been unfailingly kind to her. Many a time when it had been hard for her to make ends meet on the low wage that David got from his work at the docks Edwin had helped her out with money. But more than that, he had always shown her sympathy and respect. Sheila owed him a deep debt of gratitude for that.

Her entry into the Ashton family had not been altogether propitious. She and David had married young because they had had to; their eldest child, Peter, had been on the way. This was something, Sheila felt, that her mother-in-law and Margaret would never quite forgive and forget. But Edwin had never seemed to hold it against her. Sheila smiled her complicity at him across the hall and quietly closed the kitchen door again.

Edwin's arrival surprised Margaret every bit as much as he had hoped it would.

'Dad,' she said in alarm when she saw him, 'you're too early.'

'Too early?' said Edwin in mock innocence. 'What time is it, then?'

But Philip had seen that Edwin was alone and he laughed.

'Don't worry,' he said to Margaret. 'He's pulling your leg.'

'All right, then.' Edwin admitted it. 'Don't panic, your

mother's not here.'

'What a relief,' said Margaret. 'Where is she?'

'Well, she met me off the ferry after work.' Edwin sat down in his armchair. 'We went shopping. I suffered her fussing around while I bought a new jacket, and that was a sacrifice, believe me.' He laughed. 'Anyway, now she's visiting the sick. I've left her at old Mrs Parker's, and if she can't keep her talking for half an hour I don't know who can. I've promised her I'll have tea ready for seven o'clock, by the way.' He patted himself on the chest and beamed round at his family. 'Am I a genius or am I not?' he said.

Freda gave her father a hug. 'Ooh, isn't he just full of himself?' she said.

'The fibs I've told for you lot, this afternoon,' Edwin said. 'We'd have had tea in the Troc if I hadn't made myself sound the meanest man in creation.'

'Has she remembered it's your anniversary?' Freda asked.

'Not a bit of it! I'm very, very hurt as a matter of fact.'

'Oh, Dad,' said Freda, 'stop being sorry for yourself. You sound just like our David.' She stopped guiltily and looked round to see if Sheila was within earshot. Quietly Philip walked over and closed the serving hatch that led through into the kitchen. As far as possible the family tried to hide from Sheila their disapproval of David's fecklessness.

When the girls went into the kitchen Edwin got up from his chair and went over to where Philip was folding the serviettes that Margaret had bought.

'What is it?' he asked, indicating the paper shape that Philip had made.

'A Bishop's hat.' Philip, concentrating on pushing one corner of the folded serviette into the other, asked: 'Did you get a paper?'

'Too busy deceiving your mother, son,' Edwin said.

'I caught a bit on the news about Czechoslovakia,' Philip said.

'Yes.' Edwin sighed. 'Well, it keeps getting nearer, doesn't it?'

Philip looked hard at his father. 'Do you know, Dad,' he said, 'That's the first time I've heard you definitely say that you think war's coming.'

'Well, we have to face up to things, don't we?' That, from

Edwin, was unexpected. One of the things that annoyed Philip about his family was the way in which they avoided talking about anything that troubled them.

'I wish I thought that was what Chamberlain was doing,' he said.

Edwin was characteristically cautious. 'I think he's doing right. It's his job to avoid war if he can.'

'Yes, Dad,' said Philip, 'but what I do is look at the facts. And when I look at the facts I see war. I can't see any hope anywhere.'

Edwin searched for a way to change the subject. Normally he enjoyed talking with Philip; he liked to sharpen his mind against his son's. It was a source of great pride to him that Philip had won a scholarship to Oxford. Edwin himself had left school at thirteen. As a miner's son he had not had the chance of much education—that was one of the reasons why Jean's family had not welcomed him when he had courted her. He was shrewd and honest and hard-working and had taught himself a great deal—enough at any rate to make himself, in fact if not in name, manager of his brother-in-law Sefton's printing works. But in spite of what he had accomplished he still felt the lack of a formal education. Because of that he respected Philip's opinions.

But this evening was not the time to talk politics. Already Philip had begun to be gloomy. Edwin held out the crumpled serviette he had been working on. 'I seem to be making rather a pig's ear of this,' he said.

Freda pushed open the kitchen hatch and stuck her head through.

'Is old Sefers coming?' she called out to Philip. Edwin, out of her line of vision, looked up.

'And who might that be, young woman?' he asked. Freda stood on tiptoe and leaned further through the hatch so that she could see her father. Her eyebrows were raised and her mouth pursed in mock alarm. 'Oh, sorry, Dad,' she said. 'I didn't know you were there.' She winked at Philip as she drew back before she closed the hatch. Edwin was sufficiently old-fashioned to think that his children should refer to their uncle by his proper name.

Not that Edwin really respected Sefton Briggs any more than Freda did. He knew him to be a harsh employer and a hard man. But the economic facts were such that Edwin had no choice but to work for him. Sefton had inherited a business; Edwin had only his skill to sell where he could. In these days and in the days when Edwin's children were young, skill was not easy to sell. It was only because of Sefton's relationship with Jean that Freda and Philip and the others had been brought up in the security that they took so much for granted. That was the bitter fact that Edwin had had to accept for years now.

Now Edwin asked: 'Is it true your Uncle Sefton's coming?'

'Yes,' said Philip. 'Him and Tony. Margaret's asked them for mother's sake. You know how she feels about her family.'

Edwin gave up his second attempt to fold a serviette. He screwed the ruined paper into a ball and held it in his clenched fist.

'It's Reg Clarke's funeral tomorrow,' he said.

Philip looked at him blankly, unable to see the connection.

'Reg Clarke? The manager at the works?'

'Yes.'

Margaret came bustling in. 'Dad, go and carve the ham, will you? Sheila's just getting it out. And Philip, find me a space for the trifle. It's nearly seven o'clock.'

Philip did as Margaret asked and then started to set out the serviettes.

'What's this about Reg Clarke's funeral?' he asked. 'I didn't know Uncle Sefton was all that fond of him. And anyway, he's been dying for years. Why should Dad think it makes such a difference?'

'Oh.' Margaret bit her lip. 'It's my fault really, I am an idiot.' She looked expertly over the table without stopping talking. 'The point is that now Reg Clarke's gone Dad is the obvious choice for manager. After all, he's been carrying Reg Clarke for years. And Uncle Sefton might think that being invited tonight was a kind of hint.'

'Oh, Margaret.' Philip laughed. 'Don't you think that's being a bit oversensitive?'

Margaret was still solemn. 'Dad doesn't think so, does he?' she said. 'You know how Uncle Sefton likes to wield his power . . . he never misses a chance to let us know that this is his house really and we only live in it because he lets us. No wonder Dad thinks it was tactless to ask him to come round tonight.' Margaret was getting angry. 'It makes me sick to see how Dad has to knuckle under to Uncle Sefton. He's worth twenty Seftons.'

Philip was looking at Margaret with admiration. 'Good for you,' he said. 'Now can you say you don't like talking politics?'

'That's not politics,' said Margaret.

'Isn't it? Don't you see that that's what politics are all about, or should be? That kind of unfairness?'

The front door banged and there were voices in the hall. Margaret looked round quickly and started to take off her apron.

'Is it time?' she asked Philip. 'Is that them?'

Philip listened to the voices and then shook his head.

'No. It sounds like David.'

'Good.' Margaret was pleased. 'Now we're nearly all here and we're all ready. I can't wait to begin.'

David went straight into the kitchen to speak to Sheila. He had already been to his own home and changed from his working overalls and in his best suit, worn though it was, he looked touchingly boyish and handsome. Sheila kissed him diffidently. She always felt shy when she was at the Ashtons'. Their confidence and competence alarmed her. Only when she was alone with David was she at ease. David was the black sheep of the family, the careless, carefree, uneducated one, and she loved him for it.

'Where are the kids?' he asked her.

'At my mum's. They're all right. I saw them settled in.'

'Good.'

'Do you like my dress?' Self-consciously Sheila turned in front of her husband. She was a pretty girl, still only twenty-five but already a little faded by nine years of bringing up her children on a tight budget.

David hardly looked at her. He was very preoccupied.

'Where did you get it?' he asked.

'It's all right. I didn't buy it.' Sheila was hurt by his indifference, 'I borrowed it off our Maureen.'

'Did you find out about Reg Clarke?' David asked.

'Yes, he's died.' Sheila took hold of David's coat. 'Don't ask about jobs tonight, David.'

'All right.' David was short with her. 'Not tonight. But I

want it sorted out soon. This is my chance. It's all going to be so simple now. Reg Clarke goes. Dad moves up. There's room at the bottom for a little one ... me. It'll make all the difference, Sheila.'

David was suddenly alight with hope. He was always very easily elated or depressed and now he was buoyed up by the conviction that his luck was about to turn. He put all the things he didn't like about his life down to bad luck; his menial job, his poverty, his lack of education. He never thought that he might in some part be responsible for them himself.

Sheila began to catch David's enthusiasm. Whenever he was happy, she was happy too.

'Oh, David,' she said. 'I hope so.'

'No more labouring,' said David. 'How do you think I've felt, working on the docks as a glorified errand boy while my brother was at Oxford? Once I get in at the works I'll be all right.'

There was a flurry of activity in the hall. Jean was just coming up the front path. Margaret called everyone.

'Come on, come on, Mum's here.'

Jean was delighted by the surprise that had been prepared for her. She stood in front of the table clasping and unclasping her hands, incoherent with pleasure.

'Oh,' she said, 'how lovely. What a lovely surprise. How sweet of you all. Edwin, how could you keep it from me? Thank you. Thank you all.'

The meal was a great success. At the end of it Margaret gave her parents the family's present, a set of records from the Messiah. Tony came late with a bottle of champagne but without his father. To everyone except Edwin, who could not help but worry about the reason for Sefton's absence, this was a relief. Sefton had the unwelcome habit of taking command of any gathering he was invited to.

The biggest surprise of the evening was yet to come. Jean had gathered all the family round the piano as she loved to do and Margaret was playing to them all when the doorbell rang.

Edwin slipped away from the outside of the circle to answer it. He thought the caller must be Sefton who had grown tired of his own company and decided after all to come along. But when Edwin opened the door it was not Sefton who stood outside. It was a young man Edwin had never seen before.

He was as disconcerted to see Edwin as Edwin was to see him. He blushed and stepped backwards and cleared his throat.

'Margaret?' he asked. 'I'm ... I'm a friend of hers.'

'I see.' Edwin smiled sympathetically. He thought he recognised a suitor when he saw one and he was only too delighted to welcome any young man of Margaret's. Jean and he had been thinking for some time that Margaret had devoted quite enough of her life exclusively to school-teaching.

'The name's John Porter. I've called about some concert tickets Margaret asked me to get.'

'Come in.' Edwin held the door wide. 'Margaret's in.'

John hesitated as he heard the sound of singing from the living-room. 'Look,' he said, 'if it's inconvenient...'

'Not at all.' Edwin was already holding his hand out to take John's coat. 'It's our wedding anniversary, that's all. The more the merrier.'

'I can come another time.'

'There's no need.' Edwin was leading the way firmly. 'Just dive into the scrum, eh?'

Margaret turned and looked round as the two men came into the living-room. Edwin grew more certain that John was more than a casual caller. Margaret suddenly seemed unsure of herself as she looked at John.

Because she had stopped playing the room was very quiet. Even John's hesitant voice sounded loud.

'I ... I got the tickets,' he said. 'I ... I'm not sure ...'

Margaret pulled herself together. She stood up briskly and began to move towards him. 'John ...' she said. 'Come into the front room.'

Then the stare of everybody's watching eyes reminded her of the conventions. She stopped at John's side and turned to face the rest of the family.

'Oh,' she said. 'Introductions, I suppose. You've met my father ... this is my mother. The rest...' In spite of her embarrassment she managed to smile. She pointed to each of the family in turn. 'My brother Philip, my brother David, my sister Freda. This is David's wife Sheila, and our cousin Tony.' As John looked bewildered in the face of so many people Margaret's smile grew wider. 'That's all,' she said. 'Except for Robert. He's the youngest, only fifteen, and he's away at nautical school. And this, all of you, is John Porter. Excuse us.'

When Margaret and John had gone out everybody started to talk at once. Except Jean. She caught Edwin's eye and smiled. She had the same idea as he had. She hoped they would see quite a lot more of John Porter.

CHAPTER TWO

David and Sheila caught the last bus home. Bumping over the tram lines it carried them away from the neat suburb towards older, shabbier streets and the cramped little terraced house that was their home. Shelia knew that David did not like this journey. When they got off the bus and started to walk down the unlighted back alley she was already on the defensive.

She was as aware as David of the difference between the house they had just left and the one they were going home to. But the difference didn't offend her so much—after all, she had been brought up in a street like this. What made her nervous was the feeling that David blamed her when he was, as he was so often now, disgruntled about his home and his job.

He had, it was true, had to face family responsibilities before he was ready for them. But that, thought Sheila, was surely as much his fault as hers. She remembered that night in the park when it had all begun. It was David who had taken the initiative then.

By the time she got into the living-room Sheila was in no mood for David's approaches. She pushed his hands away when he tried to draw her towards him.

'No, David,' she said. 'What do you think I am? You sulk all the way on the bus and then when we come in here ... what do you think I am?'

David tried wheedling. 'We're all right, aren't we?'

'Are we?' said Sheila. 'It's you that says whether we're all right, isn't it?'

David reached for her again. 'Come on, Sheila,' he said. 'Come on, love.' He was, as usual, beginning to win her round. But she was still cautious. 'Is it the drink talking?' she asked.

David wasn't in a mood for bandying words. He let his hands drop.

'Excuse for tonight coming up,' he said in disgust. 'I knew it on the bus.'

Now that she could see that David was hurt Sheila wanted to please him. 'No,' she said. 'No excuse.' She thought ahead. Smiling at her husband to show that she wasn't, after all, rejecting him, she ran very quickly upstairs.

She came down again more slowly. Suddenly she really was afraid of what turn David's mood would take.

'Davy,' she said, 'Davy ... there aren't any. The tin's empty.'

David was not a man to give up easily when he wanted something as much as he wanted Sheila then.

'Never mind,' he said, bringing all his considerable charm to bear. 'It's been empty before. Sheila ... love.' He was stroking the curve of Sheila's hip, confident that he would win.

Sheila broke away desperately. 'It's not safe,' she insisted. 'We can't afford ... David, we must be careful.'

David was furious. He stood back from Sheila and shouted at her. 'The tin's empty, is that it? Is that what matters? Is that what life's about? I was skint and so the tin's empty ... oh, what's the use.' He turned and ran like a charging bull out of the door.

He carried his anger and frustration with him all the way as he ran through the wet streets from his house to his old home. It was still with him when he woke the next morning in the bed that had been his when he was a boy. It was, ironically, aggravated rather than eased, when his father gave him some money. It wasn't charity that David wanted. It wasn't, either, simply that Sheila should give in to him. By morning all his desperation had become focused into one aim. He must make a fresh start.

He told his mother as much while she was giving him his breakfast.

'All I want is a job at the works,' he said. 'A proper job, one I can hold my head up in, not one a fifteen-year-old lad could do.' He put his head on one side and asked: 'Can't you get Dad to see to it for me?'

'Why don't you ask him yourself?' Jean said.

'I can't. I asked him once and he said it wouldn't do. Said it wasn't right. I'd stand a better chance if I was a stranger sent from the Labour.'

Jean sighed. It wasn't the first time she'd had to arbitrate between Edwin and David. 'He doesn't think you'd be any better off, you see . . .' she said.

'Let me try.' David was pleading. 'Let him give me the chance. He can now, can't he? Now Reg Clarke's gone, now there's room. Ask him for me, Mum.'

Jean looked with sorrow at her eldest son. Whatever his faults she couldn't help but love him. Whatever his inadequacies she wanted to help him.

'I'll see what I can do,' she said.

Reg Clarke was buried at two o'clock that afternoon. After the funeral Sefton took Edwin and Tony back to the printing works with him in his car. Making himself master, as he always took care to do on his occasional visits there, he led the way down the rickety steps into the manager's office and sat down in Reg Clarke's old chair.

The office, like the rest of the works, was shabby. Sefton was not a man to spend money on unnecessary decoration. He didn't even notice the distaste with which Tony was surveying his surroundings.

Before they could settle themselves Edwin was called away by one of the men to deal with a problem. Father and son were alone.

'Was this Reg Clarke's office?' Tony asked. He worked at his father's other venture, the shop, and hadn't been in this back part of the works since he was a boy. He was surprised at how small the room seemed now.

'That's right.' Sefton looked round gloomily. 'He was a good practical printer in his time, was Reg. You could leave him to get on with it. And he kept the compositors in their place. Your Uncle Edwin's a bit free and easy for me.'

'Oh.' Tony sat down on the edge of the cluttered desk and crossed his arms. 'I thought Uncle Edwin had been practically running the place for quite some time.'

Sefton looked sharply at his son. 'He's too free and easy,' he said with emphasis. 'And I've a feeling his politics are best not talked about as well. He was a firm hand was Reg, in his day, and that's what's needed.' Sefton folded his hands across his waistcoat and leaned back in the chair. 'What you see here, lad, is your grandfather's estate . . . plus a few houses here and there. It keeps your grandmother in her nursing home, and when she's gone there'll be a few quid for a few people, but that's all. The store's where the real profit is these days and that's all mine, lad.' Sefton puffed out his cheeks. 'All mine.'

Edwin knocked on the door and made his way down the narrow steps.

'Sorry I was a long time,' he said. 'But I had to ring the block-makers.'

'That's all right,' said Sefton. 'Can't afford to stand still. Tony.'

'Yes, Father.'

'Take a walk round the works, there's a good lad. Show the family face.'

Tony got to his feet as slowly as he dared. His dislike of his father showed in his face, but, man though he was, he was still too much in awe of Sefton openly to defy him. They had spent too many years together, they had fought too many battles, for Tony ever to take his father lightly. It would be some time yet before Tony had the courage to go against him.

'I take it you'll blow a whistle when you want me,' he said, and went.

Sefton turned his attention to Edwin.

'Well,' he said. 'This is a bit of a setback. He's left a fair-sized hole behind him, has Reg.'

Edwin looked warily at his brother-in-law. Over the years he had gained some skill in gauging Sefton's mood. Sefton was never direct, that wasn't in his nature, but sometimes he was more devious than others. Edwin had the feeling that that afternoon, at any rate, Sefton was going to avoid doing the obviously fair thing. He wasn't, after all, going to be able to go home to Jean that evening and tell her that he had been appointed works manager.

Sefton didn't even seem to notice Edwin's silence.

'The point is,' he went on, 'what are we going to do?'

Edwin found his voice. 'Carry on, I suppose.'

Sefton shrugged. 'This place is barely paying its way, you know.'

This was Edwin's chance. 'There's too much time wasted on maintenance,' he said. 'I think you'll find that a couple of new flat beds could be an economy in the long run.'

Sefton cut across him. He always shied away from anything that might mean spending money.

'The clients will miss him,' he said. 'Reg, I mean.

'They've got used to me now,' Edwin said.

'How do you mean?'

'I've been doing most of the calling recently.'

'Good, good.' Sefton got to his feet, suddenly in a hurry to go. 'Then you can carry on as you are, can't you? For the time being, that is. That would be best.' He looked round with the air of a man who has done his duty. 'Now then, where's Tony? I shall need him to drive me home.'

When Sefton arrived at the glowering Victorian mansion where he lived he found Jean already there. She had been waiting for about half an hour but the time had passed quickly for her. This was the house that Jean had been brought up in. It was filled with memories for her.

That Jean and Sefton and their very much younger sister Helen had had a largely happy childhood was entirely due to their mother. Jean remembered her as a kind, clever, busy woman who had devoted a great deal of her energy to shielding her children from their father. He had been a figure to dread when they were small, a truly Victorian paterfamilias. It saddened Jean to remember that her mother now was reduced to a senile wreck in a Bournemouth nursing home.

Sefton's housekeeper brought a tray of tea, and left it for Jean to pour out. Sefton was glad to see his sister. He was often more lonely than he would ever have admitted. He appreciated the family link that Jean so assiduously kept up more than ever she realised.

He wasn't so happy, though, when she brought the conversation round to business.

'I thought we had a little agreement,' he said. 'No talking about the works. You have a residuary interest, the same as me, but it's worth nothing while Mother's alive, and it'll be worth nothing at all ever unless I'm left to run things my way. Right?'

But Jean, in her own way, was as stubborn as Sefton.

'That's all very well,' she said, 'but it seems to me that these days you're more interested in the store than in the works. That's fair enough in its way, I suppose. After all, the store's all yours. But Edwin gets his living from the works. It's as much his interest as the store is yours.'

Sefton was at once on the defensive.

'Are you going to ask me if I'm going to make him manager?' he said. 'That's not playing fair, is it?'

'Why not?' asked Jean.

'Well.' For once Sefton was floundering. 'Edwin's had a good living from the works ever since the day you married him. You must admit he's done very well for a working-class lad. I mean . . . I like Edwin well enough . . .'

Jean remembered a lot of things. Most of all she remembered how Edwin had been received in this house when she had first brought him home.

'Only Mother liked Edwin,' she said bitterly. She felt a surge of loyalty and love for her husband. 'You always took your cue from Father,' she accused.

Sefton, remembering too, shifted uncomfortably.

'It was a long time ago . . .' he said. 'Anyway, I might be thinking of putting Edwin up for manager. He's in the picture, of course he is.'

'As a matter of fact,' said Jean, 'that's not what I came about.'

'What was it then?' asked Sefton, relieved.

'A job for David.'

'That?' Sefton, off the hook, expanded. 'Why didn't you say so in the first place?'

'You mean there is one?' Jean asked.

'Well.' Sefton settled his hands across his stomach as he liked to do. 'If there isn't we can move one of the dead-legs down at the bottom to make one for him, can't we?'

Edwin, on his way home from work, was thinking about Sheila. Very late the previous night he had been round to see her. After David had fallen drunkenly into bed, Edwin had taken it upon himself to go round and tell Sheila where her husband had got to. He hadn't been able to bear the thought of her being alone and anxious.

Sheila, half crazy with worry, had cried.

'David's not like he used to be,' she had said. 'There seems to be something driving him all the time. He's unhappy and he's making the rest of us unhappy . . . the kids and all. That's not fair, is it? It's not their fault . . . nothing's their fault. They're only little, after all.'

Edwin had done what he could to comfort her.

'He'll get over it. It'll pass. You know David.'

'He wants a change,' Sheila said, 'that's all he talks about. He says it'll make all the difference. A job at the works, that's what he wants.'

'It won't make all the difference though, will it? It won't change David himself. It'll be much the same hours, not much more money. Can't you get him to see that, Sheila?'

Now, walking up from the ferry and remembering again the distraught sobbing with which Sheila had answered him, Edwin came to a sudden decision. Instead of taking his usual bus home he got on the tram that would take him to Sefton's.

When he arrived at the house Sefton was alone. Tony, after the usual silent meal with his father, had gone out for a drink. He had gone to escape from the company of his father. Sefton in a good mood he found boring; Sefton in a bad mood unbearable.

He had only just gone when Edwin rang the doorbell. Mrs Foster, the housekeeper, let him in. Sefton was not at all surprised to see him.

'Well, Edwin,' he said. 'Is it business? I thought this afternoon that you had something on your mind.'

'Yes, Sefton.' Edwin stood near the door, stooping even more than usual. After his late night and a difficult day he was very weary.

'Well, then, sit down,' Sefton said. 'Tell me all about it.'

Edwin rested his hands on his knees and stared down at them. 'The fact is,' he said, 'I've got a favour to ask.'

'I see.' Sefton looked almost roguish. 'Out with it, then.'

'It's about our David . . .'

For once Sefton was taken aback. This wasn't what he'd been expecting.

'She's a funny woman that sister of mine,' he said. 'She comes round here about David and asks me, all secretive, not to mention it to you, and now I see that you've been talking about it after all. You did know Jean was going to come, didn't you?'

'Er . . . no. Well, the fact is I'm just on my way home . . .'

'What I want to know,' said Sefton, 'is why she couldn't just ask you about a job for David. You've got the authority to make room, you can throw someone out. There must be somebody playing the old soldier.'

'There isn't,' Edwin said. 'Nobody can afford to, these days.'

'Well, anyway,' Sefton wasn't to be put off. 'Just make an excuse, then. Get rid of someone. You easily can.'

'No, Sefton.' Edwin's sense of justice was outraged. 'I can't do that the way things are in the labour market these days. All my men are good workers. They have wives and families to keep. I can't just give them the sack for no good reason.'

Sefton shrugged, impatient with Edwin's scruples.

'At least David has some kind of a job,' Edwin went on. 'Not just what he wants, perhaps, but it keeps him. If I dismiss someone from the works they'll have nothing.'

'Please yourself,' said Sefton.

'There are other ways.' Edwin was now in a wretched position. He had at all costs to avoid asking outright for Reg Clarke's old job and yet he wanted to make it clear to Sefton what the position was. 'If there's a move round . . . if there's a shift up . . . there would be room at the bottom then. If that did happen . . . if there was room, would you object if I gave a job to David then?'

'All right.' Sefton was tired of the whole business now. 'You could do what you liked. I wouldn't object, no.'

'Thank you, Sefton.' There was no point in Edwin staying longer. He would get nothing further out of Sefton this evening. 'I'll be on my way, then.' Edwin couldn't wait now to get back to the comfort and company of his own home. 'I'll say good night.'

David, his shirt off, was washing himself at the sink in the tiny scullery of his home. He was in an ebullient mood.

'New Brighton on Sunday, then?' he said.

'Who?' Sheila asked.

'Us. Day out for the Ashton's.'

'You haven't told the kids?' asked Sheila sharply.

'Now then!' David reproved her. 'Think I'll disappoint them, do you?'

'What if we can't afford it?'

David laughed out loud. Nothing could depress him this evening. 'Get single fare, then,' he said. 'Swim back.'

'How can you be so sure it'll be all right, David?'

'Because . . .' David had finished washing now and he came up close to Sheila. 'I called to see Mum on my way home and she said . . . perhaps. And Dad wasn't back. He was late, and do you know why I think that was? He'd gone to see my uncle. It'll be all right. Don't you see, Sheila, it'll be all right. Dad'll see me right . . . smile for me, Sheila.'

And Sheila, as carried away as he was, turned into his arms.

Tony did not leave The Plough until closing time. He expected that by then his father would be in bed, but when he got home Sefton was still sitting in the big, dark, over-furnished living-room waiting for him.

'You've been long enough,' he said grumpily.

'Been playing darts.' Tony said. 'Very good for soothing the savage breast. When you think who you might be sticking those sharp little points into . . .'

But Sefton was too preoccupied to respond to Tony's goading. He said: 'I've got a job for you.'

'What? At this time of night.'

Sefton did not bother with preamble or gloss. With the bluntness that he, knowing no better, mistook for honesty, he said: 'I want you to be manager at the works.'

There was a sickly silence as Tony took in the implications of what his father had said. The incredible unfairness to Edwin of such an appointment surpassed anything that even Sefton had ever done.

'Now just a minute,' Tony said.

Sefton smiled with the bland confidence of a man who knows that his is the position of power.

'You've got objections?' he said.

'Of course I've got objections!'

'You'd better get them off your chest, lad.' Sefton spoke pleasantly enough but there was in his face a hint of the steel that had terrorised Tony when he was a child. 'You start at the end of the month.'

Tony elected to carry the news to Edwin himself. He went to see him at the works the next afternoon. It seemed the least he could do. He felt ashamed that he had not stood out more firmly against his father's command, but after a searing row Tony had had to concede defeat. The plain fact was that there was nothing Tony could do but obey. The only thing he had been trained for was to work for Sefton, and his father had made it very plain that if he didn't accept the job as works manager there would be no other place for him.

Tony was kind-hearted and upright. He didn't want to hurt anyone. But he had not got the strong will of his father, and he liked his little luxuries. In the end he had agreed.

Edwin took the news bravely. That only made Tony feel worse. For a moment it seemed as if Edwin would be the one who offered comfort and Tony the one who received it.

'It's my own fault in a way, I suppose,' Edwin said. 'I've eaten humble pie for getting on for thirty years now, so perhaps it's all your father thinks I'm used to. I should have taken my chance of what else I could get when I was young, not just accepted the job here because it was in the family. That was asking for trouble, I suppose. I knew it at the time. But your aunt wanted me to take it . . . didn't want to go too far away from her mother . . . and Margaret was on the way. I was a fool.'

Tony was aghast. 'I'd no idea you felt like that.'

'No, son, not many people do. I don't often have occasion to talk about it, do I? But this . . . I'll not deny I expected to get the manager's job.'

'I don't know why he does these things,' Tony said.

'Don't you? I think I do. He's shrewd enough, you know, your father when it comes to business. He thinks I'm too soft on the men. He thinks I'd always be chasing him for money and for improvements.' Edwin laughed bitterly. 'Well, he's right too. I'm everything he doesn't want. Reg Clarke was his man through and through. I'd be too independent for him.'

'You know, of course,' said Tony, 'that you can carry on just as before. I shan't want to interfere.'

'That's as may be, son,' said Edwin. 'I'll have power without glory, eh, shall I? We shall see.'

'Dad.'

'What?' Edwin turned round sharply and Tony moved out of his way so that he could see who had spoken. David was standing at the top of the steps leading down into the office.

'What are you doing here?' Edwin asked.

'It's my dinner hour,' David said. 'I nipped over on the ferry.'

'I see,' said Edwin. He was not happy. This was something David had never done before.

Tony recognised that the situation was tricky. He was

familiar with tricky situations.

'I'll be off,' he said. 'Got an errand to do.'

David passed him on the stairs. He came to stand next to his father.

'Look,' he said, 'I don't want to push it, Dad . . .'

'Push it,' said Edwin. 'Push what?'

'Well, you know, the job.'

'What job?' It was too much for Edwin to grasp all at once. With his own hopes so lately dashed he had quite forgotten about David's.

'You know. You said you'd do your best for me. You told Sheila . . .'

'Do my best for you?' Edwin looked at David silently for a long minute. 'Well, I've done it. And the answer's no.'

'It can't be.' David was past noticing his father's distress. 'What shall I do?'

'What we all must do,' said Edwin. 'What I've been doing for thirty years. Swallow your pride. Do you think I've enjoyed doing that? Because if you do, I haven't. And do you know why I did it? For you. For all of you. To be the breadwinner. I did that but I lost something else.' Edwin's voice was very low. 'For nearly thirty years I've served . . . you know that word, don't you, David . . . served a man I wouldn't want to be the equal of. Not a villain, not a fool, just a man I consider in my terms a second-rate human being. And do you know what I've lost? I've lost a lot. I've lost my self respect.'

Even David, self-centred though he was, was moved by the strength of his father's feelings. The very fact that Edwin so rarely revealed them, the way in which he normally presented a brave face to the world, gave them added force. David put his hand out towards his father.

'Dad?' he said, 'I'm sorry. I'm very sorry.'

Edwin recovered himself a little. 'That's all right, son. Not your fault.'

'Only you see, Dad, I've got no job. I was sure, I was quite sure . . . they'll have somebody lined up by now. I gave in my notice this morning.'

By the time he was ready to leave work Edwin was feeling a little better about his own situation. It wasn't the first hard knock that he'd had to get over. But he was beginning to be worried about Sheila. He remembered her insisting how important it was for her marriage that David should have a change. The kind of change that David would now have to announce wouldn't solve anything. Edwin decided that he ought to call and see her, if only to explain that he had done his best to help her.

When he got there Sheila was just getting her children ready for bed. David had not come in. This worried Edwin. David had said he was not going back to the docks that afternoon. If he had not gone home, where was he?

Edwin waited until the children were out of the way before he broke his news to Sheila. She took it very stoically. She had come not to expect too much from life.

'It can't be helped, Dad,' she said. 'It's the way the world is, isn't it? It's always other people who seem to do all right. The tough ones, I suppose, and David's not really tough enough. It wouldn't have made that much difference anyway, in the long run. It's not just a change of job that David wants.'

Edwin was impressed by Sheila's shrewdness. She wasn't a clever girl but she had her head screwed on. She would be good for David, if he'd let her be. Edwin tried to comfort Sheila, angry that his son was not there to do the comforting.

David came in an hour later. Edwin had stayed with Sheila, not liking to leave her on her own to worry. He was not at all surprised to see from his son's flushed face that he had been drinking. What he didn't expect was to see David so cheerful.

'What's up, then?' David asked, as Sheila and Edwin stared at him. He started to laugh wildly, reeling about. 'Been to a funeral, then?'

'David.' Sheila tried to shake him sober. 'Be quiet. Where've you been? What have you been doing?'

'Been? Where've I been? I'm all right, aren't I? Look at me, I'm all right. See, I'm smiling.' David started to laugh again, his voice high and hysterical in the tiny room. 'I've been getting myself a job, that's what.'

'A job? What? Where?' Sheila shook him harder. 'David . . .'

'What job, son?' Edwin asked.

'How do you fancy me in uniform?' David said to Sheila. 'They've taken me for air crew in the R.A.F.'

CHAPTER THREE

So David went away. So, later, did Philip. David's departure was a public one: he had Sheila and the children and his mother and father to see him off. Philip intended his to be very private indeed.

All through the summer he had been thinking about what was going on in Spain. His brief sight of war had both horrified and fascinated him. He had been shocked and sickened by some of the sights that he had seen—the bombing, the deaths, the helpless misery of uncomprehending women and children. But he had enjoyed the excitement and the friendship of his comrades. He'd been buoyed up all the time he'd been in Spain by a sense of purpose and the conviction that what he was doing was right. At the end of August he decided that he must go back.

He made arrangements to leave Liverpool in the middle of the night. He knew that that was a rather underhand way of doing things, but he could not bear seeing his mother's reaction when she knew what he was going to do.

Upstairs in his bedroom he wrote a note to his father to explain everything. Then he packed a small suitcase with the bare essentials he would need. At three o'clock in the morning, carrying his suitcase in one hand and the note in the other, he crept very quietly downstairs.

Someone had left the light on in the living-room. From a long-instilled habit of economy Philip stopped to switch it off. He was thunderstruck when he heard his father's voice.

'Philip, is that you? What are you doing up at this hour?'

'I . . . I . . .' Philip cast around for an excuse. 'I saw the light on.'

'Oh.' Edwin was sceptical. 'You're dressed.' He looked closer. 'And you've got a case. Hadn't you better come in properly, son? I think we should have a little chat.'

Edwin had been sitting in his armchair reading. On hot nights like this he didn't sleep well and so he had come downstairs so as not to disturb Jean. Now he put his book down and concentrated on Philip.

'What exactly is going on?' he asked.

Unhappily Philip held out his note. 'Perhaps you'd better see this,' he said. 'You were meant to find it in the morning.'

Edwin, frowning, read what Philip had written.

'Why didn't you feel you could come and tell me this straight out?' he said.

Philip looked shamefaced. 'I suppose I thought you might try and stop me going,' he said.

'Stop you?' said Edwin. 'By persuasion, do you mean? Well, if you thought that you were absolutely right. As I look at you, you're making a wrong decision, Philip.'

Philip started to speak but Edwin held up a hand to stop him.

'Wait,' he said. 'Listen to me for once. I know there's a little voice in your head saying, "you don't have to listen, it's the older generation talking", but just this once I want you to try. I've a pretty good idea how you feel, son. I'm not without feeling myself for a country that's being abused as Spain is. But now I'm asking you to forget about feeling and try thinking instead. It's not a war you're wanting to go back to, it's a blood-bath.'

Philip didn't want to listen any more.

'So we all sit back and do nothing,' he said. 'Is that what?'

'It's too late now for anything but a gesture,' Edwin said. 'Before, maybe, you were doing some good, but now . . . it's a blood-bath. I read the papers. Atrocities . . . first one side, then the other. Doesn't there come a point when too much wrong has been done for right ever to come out of it?'

Without knowing it both the men had raised their voices. They had woken first Jean and then Margaret. For several minutes the two stood in the hall listening to what was being said. Then Margaret burst into the room.

'Is this a private debate?' she asked, with deceptive calm. 'Or can anyone join in?'

Edwin tried to cover up. 'You awake too, Margaret?' he said.

'It's no good, Dad, I heard.' Margaret turned to Philip. 'Don't you care what you do to people?' she asked him.

'Margaret, leave it to me,' Edwin said.

'I can't,' said Margaret. She pointed to Philip. He had picked up his suitcase. 'You don't seem to be doing too well at stopping him, do you?'

'Nobody can stop me,' said Philip wildly. 'I've got to go.'

'You can't go.' Margaret stood between Philip and the door. 'I won't let you. Look at Mum. Look what you're doing to her.'

Unable to bear it, Philip out his head down. He walked unseeingly into Margaret as she blocked the doorway.

'Let me go.'

'I won't, I won't.' Margaret grasped him, holding him back. Behind her Jean started to sob gaspingly as if she were choking for air.

It was Edwin, suffering as much as any of them, who made way for Philip.

'Let him go,' he said, as much to himself as to Margaret. 'He's a man, now. He must do what he thinks best. He must face it . . . we all must. Let him go.'

Philip wasn't quite a man when he went to Spain but he had become one two months later when he came back.

In the spring Margaret announced her engagement to John Porter. It came as no surprise to the Ashton's. They had seen quite a lot of him in the months following his first visit to the house, and they liked what they saw. Gradually he had overcome his shyness enough to chat with Edwin when he called to take Margaret out somewhere or to help Jean with the washing up when he was invited to Sunday tea.

It had been obvious all along that John was devoted to Margaret. Her attitude to him was not so clear. Margaret had never been a demonstrative girl and with John, at least in front of the family, she was very matter of fact. But she was undeniably happy on the night she announced her engagement, and Jean and Edwin in turn were happy for her.

Margaret wanted the wedding to take place very soon. Jean demurred a little at this.

'The middle of June?' she said to Margaret. 'So soon? It doesn't give me much time to get ready. Why not wait until the autumn? An October wedding can be very nice.'

'We don't want to wait,' Margaret said. 'Somehow I have the feeling . . . you know how much I hate all this talk of war. Sometimes I think that if people go on about it as they are doing they'll talk themselves into it. It's all so unsettling. You can't be sure of anything. If we wait till the autumn how do I know that things will still be the same? There might be a war by then, John might be in the army. I'd rather go ahead now while I still know where I am.'

'Of course, dear, it's up to you.' Jean knew that she could never prevail once Margaret had made her mind up. 'We'd better get busy then. There's such a lot to do. Dresses to buy, lists to make . . .'

'We've already made a start with some of it,' Margaret said. She produced a piece of paper. 'I wrote down all the people I thought we should have and John did the same, and then we did a bit of compromising about some friends of his mother. By which I mean we crossed off some of ours to put them on. The grand total of guests comes to forty-two. Do you think Dad can manage that? I don't want it to be too expensive for him.'

'Oh, I'm sure he can.' Jean took the piece of paper. 'I'm sure he'll want to give you a nice wedding. After all, this will be the first proper wedding in the family. Not counting David, I mean.'

In spite of the haste Jean enjoyed preparing for the wedding. She was always glad of an opportunity to gather all her family together. She wrote straight away to each of her sons to ask them to be sure to get home for the big day.

With both David and Philip she was relatively successful. David could get enough leave to enable him to be present for at any rate the first part of the ceremony, while Philip wrote to say that so long as he could bring with him one of his Oxford friends with whom he had arranged to go on a walking holiday he 'wouldn't miss it for anything'. It was Robert who disappointed her. He wrote sadly from his school to say that Margaret had picked a date that was exactly in the middle of his exams and in spite of all his efforts at persuasion his headmaster would not let him have the time off.

Jean's disappointment was softened by the tone of his letter. She knew that if Robert's efforts at persuasion had failed there would be nothing else that anybody could do to change the headmaster's mind. Her youngest son could be very persuasive when he tried.

The day of the wedding dawned, as everyone had hoped it would, bright and dry. Margaret was awakened by the sound of yells and laughter from the bedroom next to hers which

Philip was sharing with his friend, Gwyn. As soon as the sleep had cleared from her brain she sat up in bed.

She looked round the room that had been hers for most of her life. She wondered what would happen to it when she was gone. Nothing, probably. It would just be left empty. With David and herself married and Philip and Robert away except in the holidays her mother would for once be left with more rooms than people to put in them.

She and John could as easily have come to live here as with his parents until they had time to find a flat of their own. Certainly that was what Margaret would have preferred. She wasn't at all sure that John's mother liked her. Celia Porter had always been polite but she had made it plain whenever Margaret had been at her house that she wasn't at all confident that Margaret could look after John. Margaret did not relish the thought of living permanently under the same roof as a mother-in-law as critical as that.

But when she tried to suggest as much to John he had been reassuring.

'She'll make you very welcome. And it'll not be for long, Margaret. We'll look really hard for a place of our own as soon as we get time. I'm sure we'll find somewhere.'

'Yes, I know we will. But in the meantime ... I'm sure my mother and father would like to have us with them.'

John looked anxious and spoke pleadingly. 'Yes, I know they would. But I am the only child and at the moment, what with all the international news, mother does get rather anxious. It would help her a lot if we were there.'

So Margaret had agreed, and today she would be leaving her home. Still sitting in bed she listened to the voices on the landing outside, trying to guage when the bathroom would be empty. She could hear her father calling upstairs and Freda's shouts in reply to Gwyn Thomas's apparently inexhaustible Welsh voice. She was going to find life at the Porter's rather quiet.

She turned her thoughts to John. She tried to visualise herself standing beside him as she would in church later that day. She felt very fond of him. He would be a steady, solid, reliable husband. A man she would be safe with. Margaret, like many other people in that anxious summer of nineteen thirty-nine, needed to feel safe.

She had known him for just over eighteen months; not very long really. They had met at a lantern lecture in St Chad's church hall. The event had been partly a fund-raising venture for Chinese Missions and partly a social occasion and Margaret had gone along early to help prepare the refreshments.

She had been setting out rows of thick white cups and saucers on a trestle table when the vicar's son, Stuart Parker, and a strange young man who had turned out to be John had carried the magic lantern in through the far doors. Mary Jenkins, who was helping Margaret, had stopped work to watch them. 'Who's that with Stuart?' she had asked.

Margaret looked round just as the two men heaved the lantern on to the tall table that had been set ready for it. Over Stuart's shoulder she caught a glimpse of John's face, red and contorted with effort. 'I don't know,' she said, 'I haven't seen him before.'

Mary had had her eye on Stuart for some time. She leaned against one end of the trestle table and gave it a push.

'Do you think this is safe, Margaret?' she asked. 'It doesn't feel very steady to me.'

'Oh, it'll be all right,' Margaret said. 'These tables always wobble a bit. Don't you remember how the boys used to push them at the Sunday school Christmas parties to make the jelly shake?'

'Well,' said Mary, 'I think I'll ask Stuart to have a look at it, anyway.'

Margaret found a box of teaspoons on a chair and started to distribute them. Mary called out and waved to Stuart, who came willingly enough. John came too, walking diffidently a few paces behind Stuart as he threaded his way through the rows of chairs towards the girls. As Mary and Stuart crouched to inspect the underneath of the table Margaret and John were left face to face.

John caught Margaret's eye and blushed. He was so obviously shy that she wanted to put him at his ease. She held the box of teaspoons out towards him.

'Would you like to help?' she asked. 'There should be one in each saucer, unless of course we run out. Do you think it'll matter if there aren't enough to go round.'

'Oh no.' John had stammered slightly and the blush still stained his cheek, but he had looked straight at Margaret with frank admiration. 'I don't think people will mind sharing.'

After that evening John had started to go to church every Sunday morning as Margaret always did. At the end of the service each week they met in the porch or at the gate. At first their conversations were tentative. John was not a man to push himself forward. But as she had got to know John better Margaret had come to like him more and more.

It had taken John a long time to pluck up the courage to ask Margaret to go to a concert with him. Margaret was glad of that. She was not usually a girl who liked to be rushed. Had it not been for the war that everybody seemed increasingly convinced was on its way she would probably have waited several more months before getting married.

Margaret went down to breakfast in her dressing-gown. The wedding was to be at half past eleven so there did not seem any point in getting dressed twice. When she went into the kitchen Philip, who was just finished breakfast, picked up the end of her trailing sash and waved it in the air.

'Here comes the bride,' he said.

Margaret pulled the sash away from him and tied it.

'Don't be silly.'

Gwyn was sitting in the chair opposite Philip. His mouth was full of toast so that he could only nod to Margaret. She sat down and thanked her mother as she brought a plate of bacon and eggs.

'Eat it all,' said Joan. 'You must keep your strength up. We can't have you fainting from hunger on a day like this.'

'Oh, Mum.' Margaret laughed with embarrassment. 'As if I would do any such thing.'

Gwyn had finished his toast and washed it down with a quick gulp of tea. As soon as his mouth was empty he started off again, talking politics nineteen to the dozen with Philip. Margaret waited until he paused to draw breath and then asked Philip: 'Does he always go on like this?'

'Pretty well always,' Philip said. 'Even in his sleep.'

Gwyn waved a hand in denial. 'I do not,' he said to Margaret. 'That's an outright calumny.'

'You stop to eat, I'll grant that,' said Philip. 'And drink.'

Gwyn laughed. 'All right, then, perhaps I do go on a bit. But if I do it's because I need to.'

'Here we go,' said Philip.

'You know I have to,' said Gwyn. 'You've seen them the same as I have, those toffee-nosed snobs up at Oxford. There's a lot more of them there than there are like me so I have to keep talking to keep my spirits up.'

'What's he going on about?' appealed Margaret.

'It's the old story,' Philip said. 'The miner's son versus the upper classes. Still, there's a lot in what he says.'

'Oh, I don't think so,' said Margaret, secure in her niche. 'Gwyn does overdo it.'

'I'm not so sure.' Philip was on Gwyn's side now. 'Gwyn had a pretty awful experience last week . . .'

'Last week?' said Gwyn. 'Never mind about that. Let me tell her what my dad's been through.'

'No, Gwyn, tell her what happened to you.' Philip was firm. 'If you don't, I shall.'

'Oh, all right, then.' Gwyn was secretly pleased by Margaret's attention. 'You tell her, if you want to, Philip.'

'Well, then,' said Philip. 'Last week Gwyn ended up in six feet of water just for saying the kind of thing he's been saying this morning. He might have drowned.'

In spite of herself Margaret was interested. 'How did it happen?' she asked.

'We were in a pub,' Philip said. 'We went there to meet David as a matter of fact. Gwyn here got involved in something of an argument with some of the upper classes and later that night they came in a gang to get him. Four on to one, of course. And he ended up in the lake. It was their idea of a joke.'

'A joke?' Margaret was horrified. 'It doesn't seem very funny to me.'

'You're so right,' said Gwyn. 'It wasn't funny at all. Now do you see what I mean . . .'

Jean came to take Margaret's empty plate. She cut across Gwyn before he could get going again.

'Come on, Margaret,' she said. It's time you got into that bath. It'll take you a long time to get ready and you don't want to be late. And as for you boys, will you remember that I don't want any of your political talk today? We had enough of it last night when Uncle Sefton was here. This is Margaret's day.'

The morning passed quickly. Everybody in the house was

busy. Freda and John's cousin Molly, who were to be the bridesmaids, fussed about their pink dresses until Jean sent them upstairs out of the way. Philip and Gwyn spread maps over the dining-room table and tried to plan a route for their holiday until Edwin put them in charge of the distribution of flowers. David, smart in his R.A.F. blue, came round with Sheila, and their excited children ran everywhere adding to the chaos.

Margaret wandered about aimlessly, clutching her old dressing-gown around her. She had a new one upstairs in her suitcase ready for going away. She felt strangely remote from everything that was happening. She found it difficult to believe that all the excitement was on account of her.

At last it was time for her to dress. Freda went upstairs to help her. She went to Margaret's cupboard and reverently lifted down the long white satin dress that Margaret was going to be married in.

'Isn't it lovely?' she said. 'I wish it was mine.'

Margaret smiled. 'Your turn will come soon enough.'

'First that asks,' said Freda.

Margaret started to peel off her dressing-gown. She slipped out of it slowly, like a snake shedding its skin. Downstairs the front door banged and she heard Sefton's booming voice.

'You'd better get a move on, Margaret,' said Freda cheekily. 'Uncle Sefton's come to see if we're up to scratch.'

In spite of herself Margaret laughed. Her tension eased a little and she started to wriggle into her dress.

'You'd better go down, then,' she said. 'He'll be expecting you to be all lined up ready to march through the door at his word of command.'

Freda handed Margaret her head-dress and then stepped back for a long appreciative look at her sister. Her normally smiling face was solemn.

'You look lovely, Margaret,' she said, 'and I hope . . .' Impulsively Freda stepped forward to kiss Margaret on the cheek. 'I hope you'll be very happy,' she whispered.

Jean came in to usher Freda away. Behind her Edwin's voice echoed up the stairs. 'Jean, the car's here. Sefton's waiting for you.' For a brief moment Margaret clung to her mother, but carefully so as not to disturb her veil. Jean patted her shoulder.

'Mustn't be late,' she said. 'See you at the church.'

Margaret took a last look round her room. Then she went out and closed the door. Downstairs in the hall there was a last-minute panic as Jean hunted for her key and Freda complained about her tight shoes. Then they were gone. For the first time in days the house was absolutely quiet.

Margaret walked slowly downstairs to where her father was waiting. He smiled up at her.

'Well, that's everyone gone but us,' he said.

'Yes.' Margaret went through into the living-room. Her pristine white dress seemed out of place among the shabby furniture. Edwin sensed his daughter's uncertain mood and tried to reassure her. 'You're looking very lovely,' he said.

'Thank you.' Margaret felt a sudden surge of fondness for this slow steady self-sacrificing man who was her father. She searched for words to express her gratitude, for a means of showing him that she had at least some idea of how much he had forsworn his own inclinations, how much he had humbled his pride for the security of his family.

'I suppose this is a good time to say thank you for everything . . .' she said.

Edwin smiled at her. 'If there were any need.'

'I think there is.'

'You'd better thank your mother, then. It's the woman who makes the home.'

'It's the man who provides it.'

The room was warm but Margaret shivered. 'What's the matter?' Edwin asked.

'Nothing.' Margaret tried to smile. 'The sun's gone in.'

'It'll come out again.'

Margaret searched for words to tell her father of the fear she suddenly felt for the future. 'I nearly gave you all a nasty shock last night,' she said. 'I nearly called it off.'

Edwin understood what she meant. 'You wouldn't be a natural woman if you didn't have a few doubts and uncertainties, love,' he said. 'Especially at a time like this.'

'Mmm.' Margaret hesitated. She was restless, keyed up for the purr of the returning car though it was too soon yet for it to come.

'Your buttonhole.' Margaret picked up her father's carnation from the table and stripped away the fern that surrounded it. 'I don't know why they always do them like this. It's in terrible taste. Here, I'll pin it on.'

Edwin looked down to where his daughter's hands pulled at his lapel. Then he looked at her face, into her eyes. 'What is it, love?' he asked. 'What are you trying to tell me?'

'I don't want children, Dad,' Margaret said. 'Not if there's going to be a war. I just couldn't cope, not with John away.'

'Nonsense.'

'I couldn't, Dad.'

'Margaret,' Edwin spoke very seriously. 'You're going away from us now. You're not the type to come running back to mother and you won't want to anyway.' He paused to give weight to his words. 'But if you're ever in trouble, love, well, we're here, aren't we?'

'Thank you.'

The doorbell rang shrilly. The mood was broken. Edwin straightened up. 'The car's here,' he said.

'I'm ready.'

'Sure?'

'Yes, quite sure.'

The gothic interior of the church was unusually bright. Sun shone through the stained glass windows and the coloured dresses of the women and the pink faces of the men decked the pews like flowers. Margaret smiled encouragement at Freda and Molly, and drew in her breath. The organ pealed and she took her father's arm. Slowly she walked through the meadow of her guests towards her future husband.

John turned as she reached his side. 'All right?' he whispered. Margaret nodded mutely. She couldn't speak. John was so pressed and sleeked and polished that he seemed different from the John she knew; she herself, in her unfamiliar satin and tulle, felt different. The words of the marriage service boomed out. They were beautiful and she had studied what they meant yet somehow now they didn't relate to her. She tried to concentrate. She reminded herself that this was the most important moment of her life. But her feeling of detachment persisted, it was as if her real self had left this trembling bedecked body that stood at the centre of the ritual. She was astonished to hear the clarity and steadiness of her disembodied voice as she made her vows.

When they got outside the church the atmosphere was like a

fairground. People stood about in groups, apparently all talking at once. Children ran at random between them. Sefton came into his own; he had persuaded Jean to hire a photographer whose work he sometimes used in promotions for the store and he took advantage of the authority that gave him. It was he who posed the different groups; John and Margaret first with the bridesmaids, then with the parents, finally with the whole families.

'Your mother,' whispered Margaret to John, as Jean took advantage of a pause to straighten her veil. 'Is she all right? She looks rather overwrought.'

'Don't worry.' John squeezed Margaret's hand. 'Dad'll see to her today.'

David came forward to kiss Margaret and shake John's hand. 'Time I was off,' he said. 'The R.A.F. don't make allowances for confetti-throwing. If I miss that train I'll be late back at camp.'

'All right, David, goodbye. Thanks for coming.'

'Don't let her boss you around too much John. Take care, Margaret.'

'Are we ready?' demanded Sefton. 'Just the bride and groom this time. Would you mind standing out of the picture Mrs—er—Porter.'

Celia Porter had been trying to get past Sefton to speak to John. At Sefton's rebuff she stepped back and put a hand up to her forehead; her normally pale face had flushed a dark red. Above the sound of Sefton's orders Margaret could hear her whine.

'My head,' she said to her husband. 'It hurts.'

Margaret nudged John. 'Your mother,' she whispered.

John's voice was anxious. 'She's with Dad,' he said. 'There's nothing we can do.'

'Come along, Margaret.' Sefton was impatient. 'For goodness sake smile. You don't want your grandchildren looking at this picture and asking what the tragedy was.'

At the reception Margaret relaxed for the first time that day. She found that she was hungry. Suddenly it seemed a long time since breakfast. She enjoyed seeing familiar faces round the long tables. The only absentees were John's parents. Celia Porter, in spite of Jean's concern, had insisted on going home but to Margaret, although she would not have admitted it, that was really a relief. Celia Porter was one problem she was glad to shelve until another day.

Sefton still kept his hands on the reins, ordering the drinks and organising the speeches but for once Margaret didn't even mind that. Not while John stood up and spoke so bravely and Edwin so tenderly and her mother was suffused with a glow of pride and satisfaction such as Margaret rarely saw.

The only jarring moment came during Sefton's speech. He made it the opportunity to hold forth about his country as if, as Philip wryly remarked to Gwyn, this was a recruiting drive instead of a wedding. His words upset Margaret. She didn't want to be reminded on her wedding day that her new husband might soon be called upon to go to war. Fortunately, the effects of his words were soon forgotten in the greater happiness of the day.

She and John went back to the Ashtons' to change. John's suitcase was already there. Because they were the first to go back Edwin had given John his key. It seemed strange to Margaret to watch John struggle with what to her was such a familiar lock. She wanted to help him but she held herself back. She had already realised that marriage changes quite a lot of things.

At last the lock clicked and John pushed the door open. He bent down and kissed her. 'Well, Mrs Porter, shall I carry you over the threshold?'

'I don't know. Shouldn't it be our own place?' Margaret regretted what she had said as soon as the words were out. John's characteristic flush stained his face.

'I'm sorry we haven't been able to get a place of our own,' he said, 'but it won't be long, I promise you.'

Margaret put a finger on his lips to silence him. 'Now. You know I don't mind. Anyway, it isn't your fault. There hasn't been time. I'm the one that's to blame, for rushing you into this.'

'Oh, Margaret, never say that. I never thought I'd be so lucky . . .'

'Well, then. That's all right.'

In the sitting-room they embraced.

'At least you've stopped trembling,' John said.

'Was I trembling?' Margaret asked.

'I could feel you beside me in church. I just wondered where my cool, self-possessed Margaret had gone.'

'Is that how I seem to you?'

John looked down at her gravely. 'I thought—when I first saw you—there's one who knows her own worth,' he said. 'I wondered then what sort of a man could make an impression on you. And lo and behold, it turned out to be me. Or at least, I thought it had.'

Margaret very much wanted to give John the reassurance that she herself had previously sought from her father but she could not find the words. So instead she reached up her hand and stroked his cheek.

'Be patient with me,' she said.

John bent his head to kiss her. 'Love,' he said. 'I'm going to be patient with you for the next forty years.'

CHAPTER FOUR

The Ashtons were not having a peaceful time in the afternoon after Margaret's wedding. Jean faced Philip across the kitchen table.

'Philip, what is going on? Where is Gwyn, why isn't he here? I know that something's wrong. Your father's not himself.'

'Well, you know, Mother, he's lost a daughter and gained a son. You can't expect him to be unaffected.'

'Philip!' Jean was sharp. 'Don't pull the wool over my eyes. Where exactly is Gwyn? You can at least tell me that. After all, he is my guest.'

Philip fiddled miserably with the edge of the tablecloth.

'Shall I put the kettle on?' he asked.

'Not until you've answered my question.'

'I don't know where he is, then.

'You don't know? What do you mean, you don't know? Why didn't you bring him back from the reception? You've surely not left him to make his own way.'

'He went off. He wanted to. For a walk!'

'You've quarrelled, haven't you, Philip? What was it about? You must tell me. I feel responsible for him. After all, he is my guest.'

'All right.' Philip sighed and rubbed his hair. 'You'll find out from somebody I suppose so it may as well be me. At least I can give you my version. Not doubt it'll all sound different from Uncle Sefton's point of view.'

'Sefton? Oh no. He hasn't been causing trouble with your Uncle Sefton. When I specially asked . . .'

'Don't blame Gwyn, Mother,' Philip said. 'He feels awful about it, I know he does. And to be honest he didn't really say anything that didn't need saying. In fact it all should have been said a long time ago. He did speak a little vehemently, I'll grant that, and perhaps the drink had gone to his head. But what he said was true.'

'Never mind defending him. I know your views, Philip, and you know that I don't altogether go along with them even if your father sometimes seems to. So just tell me what was said.'

'I suppose it started off with that machine guard. The one Dad said he needed for the old printing machine down at the works. It is a legal requirement to have them now and I know Dad's been worried about it but of course old Sefton did nothing about it until he was compelled to. Anyway, there he was, leaning on the bar blaming the inspector's visit on to a chap called Morgan, and saying he was going to have him out. Think of it, Mum, giving somebody the sack simply for asking for their rights, when the labour market's like it is now. Anyway he was twisting Dad's arm about this, and Tony's too, when Gwyn stepped in with a few home truths. You know, about changing the system and so on. Plus a few personal remarks about Uncle Sefton riding roughshod over people.' Philip stopped as he saw his mother's face. 'I'm sorry, Mum, don't be upset.'

'How can I not be?' Jean sat down and put her head on her hands. 'On a day like today when we're all together and I thought it was all so nice and familyish.'

'Don't worry about it. It's only a little thing. Not the most important thing that's happened today, is it?'

'I suppose not. But still, your father and Sefton . . .'

'It's Gwyn that's in the bad books, not Dad, for once. Perhaps it's as well, come to think of it. What would have happened if he hadn't intervened and it really had come to a straight yes or no between Dad and Uncle Sefton about sacking Morgan?'

'Philip, I hate it when you talk like that,' Jean said. 'Of course your father wouldn't dismiss a man unfairly, but then neither would your uncle insist on it. I know he sometimes sounds a little harsh but that's not the real Sefton, I know it's not. He's been kindness itself to all of you, you must say that. Sometimes I think he puts on a stern face that isn't him, I don't know why.'

'I daresay you're right, Mum. If that's what you think ... After all, he is your brother. Tell you what, I'll put the kettle on for you and then I'll go and look for Gwyn. Just forget about it, that's best.'

'All right. Thank you, Philip.'

Jean sat with her head in her hands while Philip filled the kettle and lit the gas. She was still in her wedding finery. When he had gone she picked anxiously at a loose thread on her skirt and got up to put on a pinafore. But then instead of reaching down the teacups she sat at the table again, oblivious while the kettle behind her came up to a bubbling boil and started to pour out clouds of steam. She could envisage the scene that Philip had described only too well. Little, dark Gwyn, purple with rage, lashing out at anyone who seemed more complacent or more privileged than he thought they ought to be. Her nephew Tony, he who had been such a pretty, outgoing little boy but who had recently adopted a pose of detachment and disenchantment standing by, taking no part. Edwin, trying as always to be the conciliator. And Sefton. Angry. Self-righteous. Hard. But often, it seemed to her, as much hurt as hurting.

Jean knew that none of her family agreed with her estimate of Sefton. But then she told herself that none of them had known him as she had when he was young. He had been different then. Often gay and sometimes loving, and very tender to their mother. But as he had grown older he had grown harsher. In fact he had become, Jean was forced to confess, more like their father.

Although Sefton had never got on with his father that did not seem to stop him emulating him. Jean had hoped that once their father was dead and no longer able to dominate Sefton with his potent mixture of bullying and calls to filial love, this harshening process of Sefton's would cease. But it had not. It was as if the old man had stamped his mark so hard on the growing boy that even when he was no longer there to apply the pressure the die still went on sinking deeper. But Jean did not forget the gentler Sefton she had once known. She, if only she, thought that sometimes she could see him still.

Sefton was one of the things that she and Edwin did not discuss. Sometimes Jean was afraid that even after all these years some of the old antagonism between her brother and her husband still lingered. Sefton had not wanted her to marry Edwin. In this too he had aped their father.

'He's not good enough for you,' they had said. 'A miner's son! He'll not give you what you've been used to, you know.' But Jean was as stubborn as they were and with her mother's support she had persisted until they gave in and let her marry as she pleased. Sefton had seemed to accept his defeat well and had found this house for Jean and the job for Edwin. Jean was grateful to him for that. She preferred not to think about whether Edwin's gratitude was as unalloyed as her own.

Edwin pushed open the kitchen door and flapped his hands in the steam. 'Jean? Are you there? What's the matter? The place is steamed up.'

'I'm sorry, I forgot the kettle.' Jean got to her feet and turned off the gas.

'I wondered where that cup of tea had got to. Philip said you were making one so I was sitting there with my tongue hanging out. What's up?'

'Nothing. Lucky the kettle didn't boil dry.'

'It's not like you to sit there and let it. What's the matter?'

'Nothing. I just forgot.'

'What? In this fog. Come on, Jean.'

'Well.' Jean was setting out the milk and sugar with meticulous neatness. 'Well, Philip told me about Gwyn and Sefton.'

'Oh did he. Wait till I see him. He had no need.'

'I asked him. I made him. Anyway, I'd have found out, wouldn't I?'

'I suppose so. Anyway, you're not to worry about it. It was a storm in a teacup.'

'Are you sure?'

Edwin nodded. but without conviction. 'Sefton will have forgotten about it by tomorrow. And so shall I.'

'Are things all right, Edwin, down at the works? With you, I mean, and Sefton. Now that Tony's there.'

'The same as they've always been. Tony doesn't take much

part really. He's a funny boy in some ways. And Sefton doesn't come round all that often.'

'Are you happy, then?'

'I told you. The same as ever. I suppose if I've jogged along there for twenty-five or so years I can manage a few more, can't I?' And Jean had to be content with that.

Gwyn came back in the late afternoon. Freda let him in. She was the only one of the family who was comfortable with him after what had happened. Edwin was the most ill-at-ease. He brushed off Gwyn's attempts at apology, saying that a little bit of outspokenness was soon forgiven and forgotten, but in truth the incident had spoiled his day. What he wanted to remember was Margaret's face as she had confided to him her fears or his own feeling of pride as he had escorted her down the aisle.

But in fact his mind was filled instead with the image of Gwyn standing up to Sefton. Saying the things that he, Edwin, ought to have said. Things indeed that he might have said twenty or thirty years ago. But now he was too tightly caught in the mesh of his years of subservience to Sefton, by the obligation to support his family and by his love for Jean. He would never speak out now. He would continue to prevaricate. He would mitigate Sefton's harshness, continue to be the kind manager standing between Sefton and the men and that was neither easy nor valueless. Even so Edwin could not help regretting the fire he had lost. Gwyn's presence reproached him and he was glad when Gwyn mumbled some excuse and went upstairs with Philip.

In Philip's bedroom Gwyn started to pack his rucksack. Philip sat down on the other bed and stared at his shoes. Eventually he said: 'Why are you doing that now?'

'I'm thinking of going tonight.'

'What about the holiday?'

'I don't think that would be a big success any more, do you? You really think I've gone too far this time, don't you?'

'Not with Sefton. He asked for it, and besides, it's water off a duck's back with him. What I can't forgive you for is the way you humiliated my father.'

'I'm sorry if I did. He's a nice man. But why are you so sure I did?'

'Oh,' said Philip, 'because I saw his face. I've known him a long time, remember. And because I know the position he's in. It's easy for you with your black and white. You take a five-minute look at his life and make it seem all greys, all unworthy cowardly compromise. What you don't realise is that there are reasons for his compromise, and that in any case that's what life is for most people.'

Gwyn buckled up his rucksack and heaved it onto his shoulder.

'You giving in already, then?' he asked. 'Settling down?'

'Not that,' said Philip, 'just being realistic, which is something I don't think you'll ever be. Besides, the way things are going settling down is the last thing any of us will be doing, I think.'

'You may be right,' said Gwyn. 'Well, I'm ready. See you at Oxford next term?'

'Maybe.'

'Maybe?'

'And maybe not. It depends. All those ivory towers will seem a bit irrelevant if war comes. I may not go back if I can find a job.'

'Yes. Well, it's up to you.' Gwyn held out his hand. 'Goodbye, then.'

'Goodbye.'

Either because the house seemed strange without Margaret or because of the tenor of the times all the Ashtons felt restless that summer. Jean felt the loss of her daughter more deeply than she had expected. She still saw quite a lot of Margaret. She and John came round at least once a week and often twice or three times, but the Margaret who called did not seem to be quite the same as the Margaret who had gone away. Mrs John Porter was quieter and more serious than the old Margaret had been. Marriage seemed to have matured her. It wasn't that that worried Jean but rather Margaret's new reserve. When Jean enquired how Margaret was managing at the Porter's Margaret's replies were very noncommital. Yet Margaret and John seemed happy enough together. Jean suspected that the difficulty lay between Margaret and her mother-in-law and resolved to urge Margaret to start looking for a flat of her own as soon as possible.

Sheila called round quite often, too. Sometimes she came

just for company. With David away she was on her own a great deal. And sometimes she had to come for help, when David did not send her any money. Then Edwin would give her a pound or two, and Jean would write reproachfully to her son.

She wondered where David had got his fecklessness from. Not from herself or Edwin, surely. Sometimes, looking at Sheila's worried face, Jean wondered whether she should blame herself. Had she spoiled David when he was a child? She had not meant to but he had been her first son and an enchanting boy. Now he was a charming man and yet, Jean was compelled to acknowledge, he had a streak of self indulgence that spoiled him. She had been disappointed and distressed when he had to marry Sheila but not altogether surprised.

Considering their unpropitious start, though, things hadn't worked out too badly between David and Sheila. Now that David had joined the R.A.F. their reunions seemed positively rapturous. Perhaps, after all, David had done the right thing by joining, Jean thought, and her misgivings about it had been unfounded.

David himself had never had any misgivings. He had signed on without any forethought in a fit of anger and despair, but when his anger faded he did not regret what he had done. Indeed, he was glad. By making a fresh start and going away from home David thought that he was leaving all his troubles behind him. It always seemed to David that his difficulties were the fault of other people, an unfair burden that fell on him without rhyme or reason. It never occurred to him that their roots might lie within himself.

He liked almost everything about his new life. He liked the camaraderie of living with a group of men. He liked the ordering of the days; it suited him to know where he must be and what he must do without having to think about it. He liked the lack of responsibility. Now everything was provided for him. And when he was free he was really free. Not bound, as he was at home, to consider Sheila's feelings or worry about his children. To David, joining the R.A.F. had meant stepping back into the carefree youth that had so abruptly and prematurely come to an end when he had had to marry Sheila.

He soon made friends. David always did. His best friend was Frank Johnson, a quiet, good-natured boy who had been homesick at first and leaned admiringly on David for support. David liked that. They shared a room and spent most of their free time together. David had been out with Frank on the evening when he had met Peggy.

The two of them had gone down together one Saturday night to a dance at the local village hall. A lot of the men from the R.A.F. station were there. It was well known that the local girls preferred a boy in blue to the men they had grown up with, a fact that caused many a scuffle at closing time. David had had a few scruples about going but they were quickly overcome. 'What are you going to do, then?' Frank had asked him. 'Stay here on your own? Come on, David. Just a dance or a drink with a girl doesn't mean anything.'

Only with Peggy it had.

She and her friend May had been standing at one end of the room with a group of other girls when David and Frank had first seen them. Some of the girls had been showing off, shrieking and pushing at each other, but May and Peggy had been rather subdued and self-conscious Frank had liked them at once.

'Do you see those two at the end,' he had said. 'The quiet ones? They look nice.'

'Well,' said David, 'it's up to you. They won't come over here, you'll have to go to them.'

'Not on my own, Dave. You'll have to come too. They're obviously together. I can't tackle them both.'

'Oh, all right, then.'

The two men had walked across the room together towards the girls. It had been by chance that they had ended up with David opposite Peggy and Frank facing May but that was the way it had stayed. The four of them soon became settled pairs; Frank and May, David and Peggy.

David did not tell Peggy that he was married. At first, because he had thought of her as a one-night stand, it hadn't seemed necessary. And after that when it was more necessary, it seemed too difficult. David wasn't a man who faced up to difficulties.

He got more and more involved with Peggy without even really thinking about the rights or wrongs of what he was doing. When he went on leave and saw Sheila and his family it was they who filled his mind. He didn't think about Peggy while he was at home. And while he was away he hardly thought about Sheila. He kept the two parts of his life quite separate.

Peggy was a nice girl. She was pretty and soft and warm and uncomplicated. She had never been far away from her quiet village. She listened goggle-eyed when David told her of the places he had been to and the things he had done. She wasn't to know that not all of his tales were true. They began to see each other regularly. At the end of a hard day she was always there, admiring and comforting. David came to depend upon her a great deal.

What he didn't at first realise was how much he in turn had come to mean to Peggy. It came as a surprise to him when she let him make love to her. It happened first on the weekend after David came back from Margaret's wedding. He and Peggy went walking in the woods together and she asked him all about the wedding. What had Margaret worn, how did the bridesmaids look, was everybody happy? Then she had clung to him and said that she loved him and told him how much she had missed him when he was away. David didn't speculate about Peggy's emotions. He simply took what was offered. It was only afterwards that he thought about how far Peggy had committed herself, and since the thought was uncomfortable he put it out of his mind.

David didn't worry about the future much at all. As the summer wore on the letters he got from his mother were more and more anxious. She asked him, as if she thought that because he was in the services he might have information denied to other people, whether there would be a war. David wrote back, to reassure her, that he thought there would not. But the fact was that he, unlike almost everybody else, hardly thought about it at all. War to him was something remote, something that happened to other people. Disaster, to him, was when Peggy told him that she was pregnant.

They were sitting in the pub when she told him. It was the last day of August and the weather was muggy. Peggy had been ill at ease all evening but David supposed that that was because he had wriggled out of meeting her parents. Peggy had been making hints about him getting to know her family for some time but he had managed to put her off, and was feeling fairly confident that he would be able to go on doing so for some time. He hadn't expected anything like this.

She dropped her bombshell right at the end of the evening, just when David was about to set off back to camp. He was due for a leave next day and had been on the telephone to Sheila to arrange it; when he got back to Peggy his mind was still half in Liverpool. So that when he took in the import of Peggy's words it all seemed to be the repeat of an awful dream. He had heard this before. He had felt this panic-stricken feeling of being in a trap before. Once upon a time, and it didn't seem to be very long ago, it had been Sheila who had given him this feeling of being stabbed in the back. Only this time things were even worse. This time he couldn't solve things by marrying Peggy.

Peggy was obviously disconcerted by the effect that her news had had on David. She stared up at him in silence and then put out a hand as if to rouse him.

'David?'

'It can't be true,' David said, as if by denying the fact he could make it go away.

'It is.'

'You've said nothing. You must have suspected.'

'I couldn't believe it somehow. I've been worried sick.'

'You can't be, Peg.'

'Can't I?'

'Oh God.' David couldn't look at her. He stared as if hypnotised at the face of the big pub clock. Peggy followed his gaze.

'It's late,' she said. 'You'll miss the wagon.'

'The wagon . . .?'

'Back to camp. I suppose you have to catch it.'

'Yes,' said David. 'I must go. I'll see you tomorrow.'

'But you're going on leave,' Peggy said.

'No, I'm not. Not now.'

'You don't have to give it up.'

'I'll see you tomorrow. Good night, Peg.'

'Go on, you'll miss it.'

'See you tomorrow.'

David slept fitfully that night and awoke with a feeling of

foreboding. He went through the routine of the morning without speaking to anyone. Solutions to his dilemma tumbled through his mind; divorce Sheila; desert Peggy; go away altogether. None of them were possible. Whatever he did someone would be hurt, and the last thing David wanted was to hurt anybody.

It was as they were collecting their breakfast that Frank said to him: 'Bad news, isn't it?'

'What? How could you possibly ...'

'No need to take it that badly, David. It's not altogether unexpected, is it? That chap Hitler's been threatening long enough.'

'You mean it's now ... what news, Frank?'

'The Germans. They've gone into Poland. I reckon this is going to be it. They're saying leave will be stopped, you'll be lucky if you get home today. In fact we'll be lucky if they let us out of here at all.'

Ludicrously David's first feeling was one of relief. If leave was stopped he would have no need to face his mother's questions or Sheila's doubts about why he had not gone home. But then on second thoughts he realised the other implications of the news. How would his mother be feeling, afraid as she must be for her sons? And what would happen to Sheila. And the children. The Government had been talking about evacuation. David resolved that Peter and Janet must go away to somewhere safe.

Gnawed by anxiety he spent a wretched day. At last he could bear it no longer. In their hut he confided in Frank about Peggy.

To his surprise Frank didn't immediately heap him with reproaches. David would have preferred it if he had. In default he reproached himself.

'Serve the bastard right. That's what you're thinking, isn't it?' he said to Frank. 'A married chap ... two kids ... come on, Frank, say it.'

'It's ... it's your life, Dave.'

'My life ... yeah, that's right, my life. Thought you were being a good mate, didn't you, keeping quiet to May and Peg about me being married.'

'I didn't think it'd come to this. I mean I thought it was just

. . . well, you know.'

'That's how it starts out, isn't it? Two of us, two of them. Only I happen to be married. She wouldn't have had anything to do with me if she'd known. She's not like that.'

'You'll have to tell her, Dave.'

'I'll go out through the gap. Tonight.'

'It's a risk.'

'How else? We're not allowed off. If you can't use the gate, use the gap. I'll go scatty if I don't see her.'

Peg was waiting in the pub. As the only man in uniform David felt horribly conspicuous. The atmosphere in the bar was very subdued. People were talking quietly, in little huddles, about what might happen. An air of waiting, of anxious desperation hung over everyone.

David put the drinks on to the table and slumped into the chair next to Peggy. He banged the palm of his hand on to the table in despair and beer slopped on to the marble top. Peggy moved his glass away from the spreading puddle and looked at David.

'What a day,' she said.

David pulled himself together. 'You all right?' he asked.

'About the same,' Peggy said. 'And you?'

'I reckon.' In the gloomy silence David looked round the pub. Peggy sipped her drink, keeping her eyes on David.

'What do we talk about, then?' she said.

'You'll have to give me time, Peg.'

'Meaning you don't want to talk about it?'

'I must have time . . .'

'Hadn't counted on it, had you?'

'You don't, do you?' David could not meet Peggy's gaze. He watched his finger as it traced circles in his spilled beer. He pressed too hard and his hand skidded slimily across the table-top.

'You hate me for what's happened, don't you?' said Peggy.

'Peg.' David looked at her helplessly. She looked so anxious and appealing that he longed to care for her. He would have liked to whisk her away to somewhere where she needn't worry any more. He struggled to find words to express what he felt. If he were like Philip he would know what to say. Except that Philip would never get himself into a situation like this.

'Don't you?' Peggy insisted.

'No, of course not.' David was wretched. 'My fault, wasn't it?'

Peggy gazed at him but her blue eyes were not accusing.

'Like a quarrel,' she said. 'It takes two.'

'Yes. Oh, Peg, I am sorry.' Cautiously David probed. 'Have you told them at home?'

'No. I'm dreading it. Even if . . .' David knew very well what she was trying to say. Even if she could say he would marry her. For a wild moment he thought that perhaps he might. That would be the right thing, to divorce Sheila, stay down here. He put his arm out to encircle Peggy, and then he thought again. He thought of Sheila, at home with his children. Perhaps at this very moment she was packing their things ready for them to go to the country, to somewhere safe. He imagined her in the little terraced house that was all he could afford to give her. He knew that Margaret and Philip didn't think much of his house. There had been a time, when they had all been children and David had been bigger than they were that they had looked up to him, but not any more. Sometimes he thought that Philip despised him. But Sheila did not. Even when things went wrong between them Sheila never despised him. He could still, by some small gesture, make her face light into a smile. He couldn't let her down. Not now, when all the world was falling into pieces.

Peggy was still staring at him. As she caught his eye her lip trembled, as if already she knew that she had lost him.

'David,' she said, 'I've got to ask.' Her voice was thin, all the life had gone from it. It sounded like his mother's on the night that he had told her why he must marry Sheila. 'If I could tell Mum and Dad we were getting married . . .' Peggy said. David's courage failed him.

'Just give me time,' he said. 'Tomorrow I'll see it's all right.'

Back in the hut Frank said: 'Well?'

'I haven't told her.'

'You've got to. That's worst of all. You can't have a girl like Peg on the end of a string.'

'I can't bear to see her face when I say.'

'You should have thought of that. A girl like Peg doesn't deserve this.'

'I never meant it to be like this.'

'I wish . . .'

'What? What is it, Frank? What's all this about Peg? What is she to you?' David looked at Frank's averted head. 'Oh, I see.' He put his head in his hands and rocked backwards and forwards, half laughing and half crying. 'What a mess.'

David's meeting with Peggy that night was brief. He didn't actually tell her he couldn't marry her, she seemed by some process he didn't understand, to have deduced it. She was very subdued when she came into the pub. She listened in silence as David tried to cheer her up. When he stopped talking she said, quite directly, without any preamble: 'Have you had enough time?'

'What do you mean, love?'

'You know. You're not going to ask me, are you, David?'

'What?'

'To marry you.'

'Peg, it's not as straightforward as that.'

'No, it isn't, is it.' Peggy seemed to have a dignity that she had not had before. 'You see David, I know you can't. I know you're married.'

'Peggy, how . . .'

'Oh, I didn't know before. I only found out this morning. You see, I told my parents. I had to, they went on and on about me being unhappy. And my dad rang the camp . . .'

'Peggy, oh, Peggy, I am sorry. I never meant . . .'

'It's a bit late to be sorry now, isn't it?'

David leaned towards Peggy but she was turned away and he could not see her face. He put out his hand to touch her but then he dared not and let it fall again. Like a blind woman she groped unseeingly for her handbag and then lurched to her feet.

'That's that, David,' she said. 'Goodbye.'

She went, leaving David staring at the slopped table-top. Automatically he reached for his beer and sipped it but it tasted flat and neuseating and he put it down again. He longed for something, anything to happen. He almost hoped for war. It would give him something to think about, something to do. Something bigger than himself to worry about.

CHAPTER FIVE

Sheila was spending a wretched weekend too. But not because of David; at least she was spared knowing about Peggy. Her fears were for her children. When David was away Peter and Janet were all she had and now it seemed that she must lose them as well. 'Send your children away,' the Government urged. 'Get them somewhere safe.'

Sheila was sure that the country was on the verge of war. Rumour was rife. Wherever she turned the talk seemed to be of gas and bombs. Sheila brooded over Peter and Janet as she got them ready for bed on Saturday evening. In their thin night-clothes they looked so vulnerable. She wanted more than anything that they should be safe. And yet the idea of sending them to live with strangers appalled her. What would she do without them?

'Peter?' she asked, as she tucked him up in bed, 'Would you like to go to the countryside?'

The child clung to her. He missed his father. 'With you?' he asked.

'I couldn't come. You'd go with the school. To somewhere . . . peaceful.'

'I don't want to go. I want to stay with you.'

'All right, all right. It was only an idea.' Sheila wished desperately that David was there to help her decide what to do.

It wasn't a cold evening but Sheila had lit a fire to cheer the dark room up. Its little window didn't let in much sun and a damp wind blew up from the river when dusk fell. Sheila stared at the flames until her head ached. Then she put on her coat and went next door.

'Will you bob in my house for an hour,' she asked her neighbour. 'The kids are asleep but I don't like to leave them. I have to go round to David's mother's. In case our David telephones, you know.'

But the possibility of a telephone call wasn't really why she was going. She was going to see Jean. Increasingly recently Sheila had sought help from her mother-in-law. When she had first married David, Sheila had thought that Jean didn't like her. She didn't blame her for it under the circumstances, but recently the two women had grown closer. Both of them sensed that as things got worse they would need all the comfort they could get.

It had always seemed to Sheila that David's family had a security that her own lacked. They seemed to be more in control of what happened to them than other people she knew were. They didn't seem to be so much at the mercy of employers and landlords and the means test. She had an unreasonable hope that even if there was a war then the Ashton's could somehow make that seem all right too.

But when she arrived at Park Road it was not the peaceful haven that she had expected. The Ashton's, too, were unsettled and apprehensive about what was going to happen.

'Who is it?' Jean called out from behind the door when Sheila rang the bell.

'It's me. Sheila. Are you busy?'

'Just a minute, until I can open the door. Philip's ladder's in the way. We're blacking out. He'll get down and move it.'

Inside the hall it was nearly as dark as it had been outside. Sheila looked round at the swathes of dark material littering this house that to her had always seemed so spacious and orderly and shuddered.

'What is it?' Jean asked her. 'Are you cold?'

'No. It just all seems so horrible. Everywhere's so gloomy. And now David's leave's been cancelled. And ... I'm frightened.'

Jean took Sheila's arm. 'Come and sit down. Philip can fix the blackout on his own. I'll call Freda and she can go outside and check up on it. Come on, Sheila.'

They settled themselves in the living-room.

'Has David phoned?' asked Sheila.

'No,' said Jean. 'He might not have the chance, you know. They may be kept very busy at a time like this.'

'Yes, I suppose so. Perhaps he will though, before I go.'

'Let's hope so.'

'Only,' said Sheila, coming to the point, 'I just don't know what to do, you see?'

'Don't worry.' Jean was reassuring herself as much as Sheila. 'It may all blow over.'

'It's the children, that's what frightens me.'

'Yes.' Jean sighed, and suddenly looked old. 'I think we just have to be as brave as we can.'

'Should I let them go? Should they be evacuated? Is that best for them? It keeps going round in my mind.'

Jean pondered for a moment. 'I think that David would want them to go.'

'Yes.' Sheila spoke bitterly. 'He'd want them to go. He doesn't see them anyway, so where's the wrench to him?'

'You wouldn't want to risk anything happening to them, you know you wouldn't.'

'I keep on hoping . . . nothing will happen, will it?'

Margaret pushed through the door backwards. Her hands were occupied with a huge pile of books.

'I've found these in the attic—oh, hello, Sheila . . . I'm collecting all the books we had as children to keep my evacuees happy. We've got more than a hundred leaving on Monday.'

'That's what Sheila's come to see about,' said Jean. 'She's wondering whether she should send Peter and Janet.'

'Oh yes, I think you should.' Margaret sat down and put the pile of books on the floor at her feet. 'Let them come with me, I'll keep a special eye on them. You can easily have them ready in time. They'll need an enamel plate and a mug each but I'll see to that if you like, Sheila. Do you know that mugs have gone up from threepence to sixpence just because the children have to have them? And they'll need their gas masks and a few clothes. Though, really, some of the poor little things are just going in what they stand up in.'

Sheila felt, as she always did, a little afraid of Margaret. Indeed, she was rather in awe of all David's brothers and sisters. They always seemed so brisk and sure. She could so well imagine Margaret with her class of children. She would be efficient and kind, but firmly in charge. She could envisage the children lined up and labelled, all carrying their few possessions with them on to the train that would take them away. Suddenly she knew for certain that she didn't want hers to go.

'Thank you, Margaret,' she said. 'But really I don't think I'll send them.'

Jean and Margaret looked at her with what she was sure was disapproval.

'Don't you think . . .' began Jean.

'They should go,' said Margaret. 'It would be best. Anyway, they'll probably like it. You should see some of the children I've got. Half of them think it's an adventure, a kind of bumper outing . . .'

'Only it isn't, is it?' asked Sheila. 'In any case, I'm sure there's no need for them to go. I won't believe anything is going to happen.'

'I tried not to.' Margaret was serious now. 'But now I'm not going to hope any more. Just prepare to do the best I can when John goes.'

'Oh, Margaret.' Jean was distressed. 'Don't talk like that. Of course it won't happen.'

'I have to face facts,' said Margaret. 'He's in the Territorials, after all. When he joined it all seemed like a game. I don't think he ever imagined himself a real soldier. I don't think any of them did. And now they'll have to be.'

This time Jean didn't deny it. The three women sat in silence, each with her own fears. Jean looked from her daughter to her daughter-in-law and then, with an obvious effort, smiled. She was deliberately taking upon herself the responsibility of cheering them up.

'We must look on the bright side,' she said. 'We're not doing any good, are we, worrying about what might never happen?'

'I suppose not,' said Margaret, but she could not smile back. 'It's this waiting that's awful. I'm beginning to think I'd rather—anything—than just go on waiting.'

She didn't have to wait much longer. The next day was September the fourth. And at eleven o'clock war was declared.

After the initial shock the news was almost a relief. The catastrophe had come and things did not after all change out of all recognition overnight. There were not enemy soldiers at the street corners, or bombs hailing down; what changes there were were on a smaller scale. The streets were dark at night; the shops were crowded as people filled their cupboards; hotels were commandeered for the business of government; the army started to mobilise. And that was all. After that first stunned Sunday people adjusted to war surprisingly quickly. Life in many ways went on just the same as it had before. The things that really made life uncomfortable were for the most part much the same things as before. And for Margaret that was her mother-in-law.

She had done her best to settle down in Celia Porter's house. For John's sake, she had determined to make a friend of his mother. She had tried to talk to Celia as she did to her own mother.

But Celia would not allow any intimacy. She was always polite to Margaret; too polite. She made it plain that Margaret was a visitor in her house. John was her own flesh and blood, she seemed to be saying, but his wife would always be a stranger.

Even so, Margaret had been happy. John was comforting and loving, and they did not spend much time in the house. Many evenings they went out together to a concert or a film or round to the Ashton's and at the weekends they caught a train out of town and went walking. And when they did stay at home John and Margaret could retreat to their own room. Margaret began to look on that one room as her home, and regarded the rest of Celia's house as though it were an hotel.

It was after John was called up early in September that things got more difficult for Margaret. John was not posted far away. He was at Formby and as the false peace continued he was allowed leave quite often. At least once a week he had an overnight pass and when he did he could be home by the early evening. It was hardly any different, Margaret and John comfortingly told each other, than it would have been if he'd got a different job across the river.

It was the other evenings, the ones when John could not get home that Margaret found unbearable.

With John away Margaret lacked an excuse to go up to her room. She tried occasionally to do so but when she got to her feet and started to collect her books Celia would ask, in a self-pitying whine that grated on Margaret's nerves, what she was going to do.

'It's not good for you,' Celia would say, 'to sit up there and brood. Stay down here and keep me company. I need somebody to keep my spirits up now that John's away.' And Margaret would be obliged to spend the evening sitting opposite her mother-in-law in the stuffy living-room making stilted conversation.

When John's father was at home it wasn't too bad. Margaret liked Harry Porter. Once she had got past his stiff, old-fashioned reserve, she found that he was a gentle, kindly man. She admired the way he behaved to his wife. Unlike John he had no illusions about Celia. And yet he was unfailingly patient with her. He could nearly always calm her when she was in one of her self-pitying moods. He seemed to be the only person who could. Certainly Margaret didn't have the knack. Margaret and Harry became unspoken allies. He seemed to sense when Margaret was at the end of her tether and would step in to her rescue.

But Harry was not always there. Like a lot of other people who were too old to fight he wanted to do what he could to help his country. The local swimming pool had been turned into a First Aid Post and equipped to give treatment in the event of a gas attack. Harry was on duty there two evenings a week. Since there were in fact no gas attacks Margaret sometimes wondered what he did to pass the time, but whether he was busy or not she was glad he had the excuse to get out. Without an excuse he could never have gone. Celia hated to be left on her own.

Margaret herself, when she felt that she really must get away for an hour or two, generally went round to her mother's. In her old home she could sink back into her old role; there she was just one of the family, not the single focus of attention, and that was a relief. But Celia resented these visits. It was as if her jealousy of Margaret extended to the whole of Margaret's family.

'What, off there again?' she would say. 'That's the second time this week. And I try to make such a nice home for you here. It's so lonely with John away.' Until Margaret felt obliged to cut down her visits as much as she could.

As the year drew on and the evenings grew longer Margaret began to feel trapped. Those nights she saw John were the highlights of her life but often Celia spoiled them, insisting on cooking John's favourite meal or monopolising his conversation, as if it were she that he came home to.

Margaret said to him one night in desperation: 'I must find a flat. Shall I start looking?' John looked more worried than ever. 'Can you wait a bit?' he begged. 'Until I know... oh, Margaret, I don't want to leave you on your own. This isn't the way I meant it to be. I wanted to look after you, make your life safe and easy.'

'All right. I'm all right.' Margaret could not but soothe him. John had changed since he'd been in the army. He was paler and thinner and more uncertain than he used to be. Army life did not suit him. He found it hard and rough. He was homesick and worried about the future. In some ways Margaret was beginning to feel that she was the stronger of the two of them. So after that she didn't talk about a flat any more. She put a brave face on. For John's sake, she decided, she must put up with her situation.

But one night she felt she could bear to be with Celia no longer. It was the middle of December and the weather had been grey and lowering all week. Harry had been out nearly every night and the children in Margaret's class at school, unsettled by comings and goings of departing and returning evacuees, had been more difficult than usual. And worst of all Margaret had a suspicion that had slowly grown to a certainty that she was pregnant.

The thought appalled her. Not because she didn't want a child. Under normal circumstances she would have been delighted. But to have a baby now was more than she could bear. It would mean more time at home with Celia. It would be someone else to be afraid for.

Margaret was sitting at the Porter's dining-table marking books. At least she was trying to mark books but her mind was wandering. She counted up the hours until she would see John. In twenty-two hours from now, she reckoned, he would be coming off the base. If she caught the train to Formby after school she could meet him there and they could go somewhere for a meal. Then she could tell him . . .

'Is it tomorrow that John has a sleeping-out pass?' asked Celia. She was sitting in an armchair by the fire, knitting.

'Yes,' said Margaret.

'I thought so. I'll make him a cauliflower cheese. You can watch me and find out how he likes it done.'

'Oh. I was thinking we might eat out. Another time . . .'

'I got the cauliflower today, as a matter of fact. He adores cauliflower cheese. He always has done since he was a little boy.'

'Oh.' Margaret gauged Celia's mood, wondering if she dared to make a stand, and insist on going out with John. Celia's mouth was grim and her knitting needles clicked feverishly.

Margaret decided that she had better not.

Celia finished off her ball of wool and and picked up another skein.

'Margaret.' Margaret pretended not to hear. 'Margaret, are you listening?'

'Yes.'

'Will you help me to wind this wool.'

'Oh.' Margaret's head ached. Celia's stare was piercing.

'It won't take long,' Celia said. 'And we can have a nice little talk while we're working.'

'All right.'

The front door rattled. Margaret dropped the wool she had just picked up and said: 'I'll go. Don't get up. I'll be glad of the . . . exercise.'

Harry was peering round the chained door. 'Can you let me in? What's it chained for? It's only seven o'clock.'

Margaret stifled a giggle. 'She's been listening to all these blackout stories.'

'I see. Thinks everyone's after her?'

'Something like that.'

'Harry.' Celia's voice floated out of the living-room. Harry looked at Margaret.

'Tell her I've just gone into the kitchen to get my tea,' he said. 'She needn't get up.'

'She's knitting.'

'Good. Better than just brooding, eh?'

Margaret went back into the living-room and picked up the skein of wool again. Celia wound her ball monotonously and complained about her husband.

'Why does he have to eat in the kitchen. He should keep us company. He never used to be like this. He used to be so smart. When I first met him, in his officer's uniform, he was so smart. You wouldn't believe how nice he used to look in uniform.'

Margaret's arms felt heavy. Since she had been pregnant she seemed to feel so tired. And yet she dared not droop in front of Celia. She must give Celia no excuse to hover over her.

Celia's voice droned querulously on. 'Did you see *The Prisoner of Zenda*? Now that was a film I really did like. No coarseness, no vulgarity.' Margaret thought longingly of her own home. She thought of Freda laughing as Philip teased her and of her mother and father smiling at each other. She stood up suddenly and put the half wound wool over the back of a chair. 'There,' she said, 'you can manage like that. I must go . . .' She glimpsed the look on Celia's face. If she said where she was going there would be reproaches. Margaret couldn't face that. 'I'm just going . . . round to a friend's,' she said. 'For a breath of fresh air. I won't be long.' She knew that Celia was aware of where she was really going, but she didn't care. Without an excuse Celia could say nothing. Even she could not accuse Margaret of an outright lie. 'Goodbye,' said Margaret, and walked quickly through the door.

Harry was just coming out of the kitchen as she reached for her coat. 'Out?' he asked.

'Yes. I must. I'm just going . . .'

'I know.'

'She's got you for company tonight. She doesn't need me.'

'I was going to go . . .'

'To the centre. Oh, I'm sorry. Were you counting on me staying in?'

'Don't worry.' Harry patted her shoulder and switched the light off so that it wouldn't beam out as Margaret opened the door. 'You just go. I understand. And first one in make sure the chain's off, or one of us'll be out all night. Right.'

'Thank you. You're . . . thank you,' said Margaret, and they smiled at each other through the gloom before Margaret walked away to catch her bus.

At that moment John was standing in a phone booth. He was cramped in the tiny space. His kit-bag leaned heavily against his leg and his gas mask banged on his hip whenever he made a move. He could not even raise his arm to rub at his neck where the rough collar of his khaki battle-dress chafed. But he dared not open the door. The tinny voice of the operator was faint enough as it was and John was afraid that if he let in any noise he would lose it altogether. And that voice seemed at that moment to be his only link with Margaret.

'Are you sure?' he said, pushing the receiver closer to his ear, 'Are you sure it's still engaged?'

'It's still engaged,' the operator said, impatiently.

'Well, wait,' said John. 'I'll try another number.' He scrabbled through the phone book. It must be Freda or Philip who were monopolising the Ashtons' phone. If only they knew. As soon as he had heard that afternoon that the unit was to be posted overseas straight away, that same evening, John's only thought had been that he must see Margaret. Because the posting was supposed to be temporary there was to be no embarkation leave; John had only two hours for his farewells and he wanted to spend every possible second of that time with his wife.

He was trying to phone the Ashtons so that Edwin could go round and warn her that he was coming. John was filled with an awful fear that he might miss Margaret. She might be out. She had no reason to wait in for him; tomorrow was the time that they had arranged to meet. If only his parents were on the phone.

John found the Brigg's number and spoke to the operator.

'Are you there? I've got another number. Try this please. There should be someone there.' Thank goodness, thought John, that he had remembered that Tony Briggs had a car.

'Hello?' Tony answered the phone. John cleared his throat.

'Hello. This is John Porter. Your cousin Margaret's husband. I wonder if you'd help. I'm sorry, it's all rather sudden. Could you go round to my parents' house? It's sixty-nine Egerton Street. I know you've hardly met them except at the wedding, but in any case it's Margaret that the message is for. I'm coming to see her. I'll be there in half an hour. Tell her to wait, please. We're moving tomorrow, you see. It's all so quick, nobody's sure why . . .'

'All right,' said Tony. 'Don't worry, I'll see to it. It won't take long. My father's got his own little stock of petrol so it's no problem. I'll have Margaret lined up for you when you arrive.'

John leaned against the side of the phone booth, shaky with relief. The thought of Margaret filled his mind. To listen to her steady voice, to tell her something of what he felt, that was what he needed to give him strength. When he had seen Margaret he would know what he was going away to fight for.

Tony was glad of an opportunity to help John. Sometimes in these past two months when he had seen men of his own age in uniform he had had an uneasy feeling that perhaps he too should be doing more than he was. Printing was a reserved occupation so he had no need to leave it yet, but Tony was uneasily aware that his presence at the works was by no means essential. Edwin had managed very well before Tony had started and no doubt he could do so again. Only the thought of his father's reaction had prevented Tony from speaking out. So in carrying John's message Tony felt as though he was in some way repaying a debt that John had undertaken on his behalf.

He drove as fast as he dared through the blacked-out streets. With only a tiny slit of light from his headlights to see by it was not easy. Other cars or muffled pedestrians had a habit of looming out of the murky night with disconcerting suddenness. By the time Tony had stopped the car three times to check on house numbers he was beginning to think that John might arrive before he did.

And after all it turned out that his journey was in vain. Margaret, it seemed, was not in and John's mother, saturnine and suspicious, said she did not know where she had gone.

'Are you sure?' Tony persisted. 'You don't know anywhere where she might be? I don't mind trying even if you're not certain. I've got the car. I can easily fetch her, if you have any idea at all. John has only got this evening. He seemed particularly anxious to see Margaret.'

It was no use. Mrs Porter insisted that she could not help. There was nothing more Tony could do.

John arrived home only ten minutes after Tony had left. He heard the front door open while he was paying off the taxi; they were expecting him. His message must have come. His kitbag felt light as he ran to the door. He still had an hour to talk to Margaret in, an hour to draw strength from her.

But it was his mother, not Margaret, who was standing by the open door. John stopped to kiss her and then walked through the hall looking everywhere.

'Margaret?' he asked. 'Where is she?'

'I don't know.' Celia had followed him. She was watching him intently. 'She was going for some fresh air, she said. She might visit a friend, she said. She doesn't always tell me where she's going, you know. So how am I to know when she won't tell me straight?'

'She's not here?' This was what John had dreaded. Every second that ticked by was shortening the time that he would have with Margaret. He must find her soon.

'I think it's terrible,' said Celia, 'sending you away like this. This terrible war. You must sit down. Rest yourself. I'll make you something.'

'No thanks. I'm not hungry.'

'But I insist. A cup of tea . . .'

'No.' Something about his mother suddenly irritated John. He found it unbearable that she should stand there so complacently while he was beginning to feel desperate. She didn't in the least comprehend his sense of urgency. 'You see,' he said. 'I must find Margaret.'

'It's not my fault she isn't here.'

'Where's Dad? He might know where Margaret has gone.'

'Ah,' said Celia, 'but he's another deserter. He's gone to the first aid post. I was here on my own.'

'He might know,' said John, clutching at straws. 'She might have told him where she was going.'

'If she did, he didn't tell me. I doubt very much . . .'

'But she might. Don't you see, I must try. I can't just sit here. I may as well go round. I'd have to say goodbye to him, anyway, wouldn't I?'

'But what about me?' said Celia. 'I'll hardly see you.'

'I'll come back.' John was already at the door. 'Just a word with Dad. I must try to find her.'

Margaret, in the Ashtons' living-room, was just finishing her cup of tea.

'Lovely,' she said to her father, 'you've saved my life.'

'It was only a cup of tea,' Edwin said.

'Not only that. You know what I mean.'

Edwin looked sharply at his daughter but thought it wiser to say nothing. He, like Jean, had noticed the shadows that had come recently under Margaret's eyes.

'When's Philip being called up?' asked Margaret.

'After Christmas, I think.'

'You'll miss him, won't you, you and Mum?'

'We miss you all, my love.'

'Do you? I miss you, too.'

'I know.' Edwin wondered again whether he should speak

out. 'Are things . . .' he began. But he had left it too late. Margaret was getting to her feet.

'I'd better be on my way,' she said.

'So soon? What about your mother? I could nip round next door and tell her you're here.'

'No, don't bother. I'd hate to upset the knitting circle. It might make all the difference to the war effort.'

'Are you sure? Believe me, it wouldn't make any difference if you held up production. The rate the ladies of this road are turning out balaclavas they'll have to supply the Germans soon, to get rid.'

Margaret laughed, and Edwin was glad to see it. 'All the same,' she said, 'don't bother. I'll be round again. Not tomorrow, because John's got a pass, but the day after probably.'

'Any time,' said Edwin. 'It's been a brief visit.'

'Short but sweet.'

'And was it only for the tea?'

'Well . . .'

'I thought so. You've got something on your mind, haven't you?'

Margaret smiled ruefully. 'I could never fool you, Dad, could I? Not even when I was little. There is something, yes, but it's John I should be telling really. I've been waiting . . . I wish he was at home tonight. Still, he'll know tomorrow.'

Edwin stood up in order to accompany Margaret to the door. He put his arm round her shoulder.

'Are you going to tell me or not?' he asked. 'You've been walking all around it. You don't have to say anything if you don't want to.'

'I know that, Dad.' Margaret kissed her father gratefully. 'You always seem to understand, don't you? The fact is . . . don't tell anybody will you . . . I'm going to have a baby.'

Edwin sat down heavily after Margaret had gone. He wasn't at all sure how to take her news. It hadn't come altogether as a surprise to him. There had been something about Margaret's manner when she had come in that had told him that something was worrying her, an extra edge to the tenseness that had come over her ever since John had been in the army.

Edwin could not help but worry about his daughter. It hurt him that the carefree girl she had been had become the anxious woman she was. And yet with her anxiety she had gained strength. Margaret might not want this baby. In view of what she had said before she was married she almost certainly didn't, and who could blame her at a time like this. But, Edwin thought, it might not in the end be a bad thing for Margaret. He had no doubt at all that when she got used to the idea she would cope. And if John were to go away, if John were to ... with a baby, Margaret would at least have something to show for her marriage.

Freda came into the living-room to look at the clock.

'Hello,' she said. 'It's so quiet in here I thought there was no one in. Margaret's gone, then?'

'Yes,' said Edwin. 'I was just taking the opportunity of hearing myself think.'

'Is that the time?' Freda asked. 'Has it gone half past eight? Whatever has happened to Tony? He told me to be ready prompt at eight on pain of not going to the dance if I was late.'

'You look very nice,' said Edwin. 'But why, if it's not a rude question, is Tony taking you to a dance?'

'Don't worry.' Freda laughed and twirled herself round in front of the mirror. 'It isn't that he's seen his little cousin in a new light all of a sudden. Just that his current—at least, perhaps, I should say his last—girl-friend will be there with A. N. Other. I'm meant to show her that she's not the only fish in the sea.'

'Oh,' said Edwin, 'I understand. At least Tony's honest about it.'

'Dad.' Freda hooted with laughter. 'It wasn't him that told me that.'

'I don't know,' said Edwin. 'The younger generation.'

The doorbell rang. Freda patted her hair. 'That'll be Tony,' she said.

'Off you go, then,' said Edwin, 'have a nice time, both of you. Good night, love.'

Edwin listened for the roar of Tony's car moving off, but it did not come. Instead, after the front door had closed, he heard Tony's voice in the hall. Then Tony followed Freda into the room.

'Dad,' she said, 'it's Margaret. Tony's been looking for her.'

'What? What for?'

'I've got a message,' said Tony. 'From John. I've just been to the Porter's but John's mother said she didn't know where she was. She didn't tell me she'd come here.'

'She's just gone,' said Edwin. 'Five minutes ago, not much more. What is the message? Is it urgent?'

'Yes it is, really,' said Tony. 'It's John. He's got to move tonight. He's to report at the railway station at half past nine. They're off just like that. He doesn't know where he's going, but it sounds like France to me.'

'In an hour?' said Edwin incredulously. 'That's . . . cruel. We must find Margaret, then, at once. You might catch her at the bus stop, Tony, in the car.'

'Does she catch the ninety-three?' asked Tony. 'I just passed it as I turned in here.'

'We must go to the next stage,' said Freda, brisk and competent. 'The bus waits for a bit in the square. We can get her there. We'll take her to the Porter's, is that best? Come on, Tony.'

'Hurry,' said Edwin. 'She must talk to John . . .'

'Don't worry, Dad.' Freda already had her coat on. 'We'll get her.'

John turned in through the shrouded door of the First Aid Post. It was the same swimming baths that he had come to as a boy until his mother had stopped his lessons and it still smelt damply of chlorine and wet clothes. But now there were no boys splashing and the cubicles were deserted. The pool of water looked vast in the dim light and the Victorian girders that supported the roof were lost to sight against the painted-over skylights. Such stillness in a place like this was eerie. Awed, John trod softly as he walked along the edge of the water.

At first he thought that there was no one there. Had he missed his father too? Then at the far end of the bath, half hidden by some boxes of supplies, he saw two figures. They stood close together, a man and a woman. John could not see their faces.

Gently they kissed. John stood still, not wanting to intrude, waiting for the right moment to ask them if they knew where Harry Porter might be. Then the man raised his head, and John recognised his father.

John didn't mean to call out. He meant to stand and think.

But somehow he heard his voice shouting, echoing in that cavernous place.

'Dad, Dad, Dad . . .'

Harry put up his hands to shield his eyes and stared across the pool. Then he said something to the woman he was with and started to walk towards John. John waited, trying to assimilate what he had seen. He was horrified by it. Not so much by that small kiss as by what it implied. What more had there been? And for how long? How long had he and his mother been deceived?

John had never thought of his father as in any way separate from his mother. He had never really thought of his father as an individual at all. So it was painful for him suddenly to discover that his father was a man like other men. The last thing John wanted on a night like this was any kind of revelation. Since he had to go away from home and from everyone he knew it seemed essential to him that what he was leaving behind should be stable, unchangeable, absolutely reliable. He was not at all in the mood to listen to his father's explanations.

Harry tried. John brushed his words aside. 'I haven't time,' he said. 'I have to go in less than an hour. Go away for I don't know how long. I've got to find Margaret. Where is she? Do you know?'

Harry looked at him. John's face was grey. Reflections off the water danced across it, distorting the line of John's grim mouth and shadowing his hollowed eyes. 'I must find her.' John reiterated. 'Do you understand? I must see Margaret before I go.'

'Have you seen your mother?' Harry asked.

'Yes. She doesn't know where Margaret's gone.'

'No?' Harry stared at his son. 'I see. Well, she's gone to the Ashtons'.'

'There? But Mother didn't say . . .'

'No.'

'I must get there. I'll go straight away. I've got a taxi outside. I can be there in ten minutes. My kit . . .'

'It's at home?' Harry asked.

'Yes.'

'Drop me off, then. I'll pick it up, and collect your mother. We'll follow you round to the Ashtons'. There isn't time for anything else.'

John was already half-way to the door. Harry had to run to keep up with him. He tried to glimpse John's face but John looked deliberately ahead. They climbed into the taxi and Harry knew that he only had a few minutes more in which to speak to his son.

'John,' he said, 'you must let me talk about it . . . about what you just saw.'

'I'd rather you didn't, Dad.'

'It isn't . . . there was nothing . . . Mrs Edwards is just a friend I'm fond of. Your mother . . . you must have noticed things. Over the years she's changed. She's not always . . .' Harry strained his eyes through the black gloom in the back of the taxi, to try and see from John's expression what he was thinking. It was impossible to explain something so painful and subtle as Celia's long-drawn-out retreat into obsessional self-regard to someone whose mood you could not carefully gauge. Perhaps indeed it was impossibly unkind to try to explain it at all to her son. In any case now there was not time. But Harry could not bear that John should go away despising him.

'I just don't want you to think that . . . that I'm an old roué,' he said.

In the darkness he sensed rather than saw John turn towards him.

'I won't tell her, Dad, about what I saw.'

'Thank you. I . . . love for one's son isn't just a mother's prerogative, you know.'

'No.' But John's attention had already slipped away from Harry back to what concerned him most. 'Will I be in time?' he said.

'You will. You'll be there very soon. You'll have a . . . a good half hour together.'

The bus was full and smelt foully of cigarette smoke and wet overcoats. In the dim blue light from the shaded bulbs the passengers were ghastly. Margaret felt sick. She wasn't sure whether her nausea was due to the atmosphere, to her pregnancy, or to her dread at the thought of facing her mother-in-law's interrogation about where she'd been but each time the bus jolted or lurched it grew worse. She felt she must have some air. She leaned past her neighbour to try and reach nearer the window and saw that the bus was just passing the end of the road where David and Sheila lived.

On an impulse Margaret stood up. She started to push her way towards the exit. She would call on her sister-in-law. Sheila, on her own, would be glad of the company, and the visit would delay the moment when Margaret must go back to Celia. Normally Margaret avoided going to David's house. This neighbourhood depressed her. The shabby rows of four-roomed houses cowered together in a maze of identical dirty streets in which gangs of children, always filthy and often shoeless, appeared to run wild. Not that Sheila's children did. Margaret did not have much in common with her sister-in-law, often they had hardly anything to say to each other, but she did admire the way that Sheila brought up her children. Margaret was not at all sure that she herself could have managed as well in the face of David's vagaries and the constant lack of money.

That evening Margaret suddenly felt a rush of fellow feeling for Sheila. She wanted to tell her about the baby. Speaking of it to Edwin had made it seem true for the first time, and the realisation had made Margaret afraid. Margaret thought that perhaps if she told Sheila of her fears Sheila would reassure her. Surely she of all people would understand how Margaret felt.

In the Ashtons' living-room Edwin was sitting opposite John, kneading his hands helplessly.

'I am sorry,' he said, 'if only she'd known. Tomorrow night, she thought. She was talking about seeing you. How could any of us have known? The army is a law unto itself. Still, I suppose there is a war on. We can't expect everything to be easy.'

'I should have had leave,' said John. 'It's only right. But with it being temporary . . . perhaps I'll be back soon.'

'I daresay you will be.'

'Only I want to see her now. Before I go.'

'Tony'll fetch her. I'm sure he will. He and Freda have gone round to your parents now and they'll see the note . . . Mrs next-door said she'd look out for them.'

'It's nine o'clock,' said John. 'I've hardly any time. I've wasted . . . hours.' He stared at his watch. It was the one his parents had given him for his twenty-first birthday. He'd been pleased with it. How many times had he looked at its dial? He had thought it an attractive watch, delighting in the clear markings of the figures against the white face. Now he hated it. The markings were too clear. They spelt out too plainly how little time he had left. He put his arm down, holding it straight and stiff, against his side, defying himself to look at the time again. His arm was stiff and his body was rigid. John sat straight in his chair like a soldier should. But it was not pride that held him so upright, it was desperation. He felt that if he gave way at all, if he relaxed even ever so little, he would collapse.

Edwin got to his feet and walked a few paces away. Then he turned again to face John.

'Son,' he said, calling him that for the first time. 'In case, just in case Margaret doesn't get here, there's something I think you should know. You can get used to the idea and then when you see her you'll know what to say. It's . . . well . . . I'll come straight out with it. She told me tonight that she's going to have a baby.'

John's first feeling was one of disbelief. It couldn't be true. This was something else on a par with all the other things that had happened on this unbelievable evening. It was all like a horrible dream. Under any other circumstances John would have been pleased by Edwin's news. But not now, not just when he was leaving Margaret. How would she manage on her own?

Edwin was looking at him with concern. 'She wanted to tell you herself,' he said. 'In fact she was just waiting for tomorrow. But tonight . . . I think she just had to tell somebody.'

'How was she?' asked John. 'How did she feel about it? We never meant . . . it doesn't seem the time.'

'She'll be all right,' Edwin said. 'We'll look after her. There's nothing you can do by worrying is there, so try not to.'

'I can't help it.' The doorbell rang, and John, still straight as a ramrod but shaking a little now, got to his feet and took two steps forward. He was breathless with relief. At last Margaret had come. At least for a few moments he could comfort her.

There were footsteps in the hall, and the sound of voices.

'Don't hope,' said Edwin, putting his hand out towards John as if to offer him support, 'I'm afraid it's not Margaret.'

John listened. The voice he heard was not Margaret's. It was his mother's. He must wait a little longer.

'No,' he said. 'It's not Margaret. It's . . . please, don't tell my mother about the baby. Let Margaret decide when . . . I'm not sure that she'd want her to know.'

'You're not happy about it, are you?' Sheila asked Margaret. The two of them were standing in Sheila's tiny scullery washing up at the stone sink. This was the first chance that Margaret had had to speak to Sheila alone as she had been longing to although she had been here for over an hour. Because it had not been Sheila who had opened the door in answer to her knock, but a rather dishevelled David.

'I didn't come to see you,' Margaret had said. 'I didn't know you were here.'

'No,' said David. 'I'm not. That is, I've just called in. I'm in transit, you might say. Moving camp.'

'Making most of his opportunity.' Sheila was still buttoning up her dress as she came downstairs and it was obvious what she meant. Margaret had felt an intruder and regretted her impulse to come. But they had both pressed her to stay so she had helped Sheila to make some supper for the three of them. During the meal David and Sheila had talked to each other with a lingering tenderness that Margaret had never seen between them before. It had made her feel lonelier than ever.

Now David was upstairs with the children. Margaret could hear his footsteps and his murmuring voice overhead.

'John doesn't even know about the baby,' she told Sheila.

'You'll tell him, though?'

'Tomorrow night. He's got a pass then.'

'What will he say?'

'Oh. I suppose he'll be pleased, really.'

'Well, then.' Sheila shook her head at Margaret as if at a child. 'What are you worrying about?'

'I don't know. I'm a bit mixed up.'

'You didn't mean it?'

'No.'

'It is a bit overfacing at first,' said Sheila. 'Even at the best of times. I should know. But you won't mind, you know, not when you've got it. There's thousands felt like you, and now they're happy.'

'Thanks, Sheila.' Margaret felt fonder of her sister-in-law than she ever had before. 'You're . . . a great help.'

David squeezed into the scullery behind Margaret.

'It was Peter,' he said. 'He was crying in his sleep.'

'He does.' Sheila dried a saucer carefully. 'He has done ever since you went away.'

Margaret put down the dish-cloth. 'I'll go and get my coat,' she said. 'Is it right you've borrowed a car, David?'

'That's right? Want a lift?'

'Yes, please. To my in-laws, remember. I'd better be getting back. It's gone nine and John's mother makes a fuss if I'm late.'

'All right. I'll have to be on my way, anyway.' David was talking to Margaret, but his eyes were on Sheila.

'Thanks.' Margaret slipped out under David's arm to let him and Sheila have a moment to themselves. She picked up her coat from the chair where it had been left and huddled into it, clutching it round her shoulders for comfort. In the scullery David and Sheila talked softly; then they were silent. Margaret yearned for John. She longed to tell him about the baby. If he was glad then perhaps she might learn to be glad. Once she had seen him smile about it, then she might begin to accept it. As she leaned against the mantelpiece waiting for David, Margaret began to count the hours until she could see John.

The Ashtons' living-room seemed full of people, and all of them were talking at once. In the middle of them all only John was silent. He still sat on his chair, straining to hear what Tony was telling Edwin.

'She wasn't on the bus. We waited at the square. Then we went to the Porters', but there was no sign. It was all dark. The neighbour said they'd come here.'

Celia clutched at John's arm. 'You should be leaving from your own home, John,' she said. 'It doesn't seem right.'

Harry bent down to her. 'Come on, Celia, let him have a minute's peace. We can go to the station with him.'

Jean held something out towards John. 'I've made a thermos for the train. Is there anything else you might need?'

John captured Freda's attention. 'Wasn't she there?' he asked her.

Freda shook her head. 'I'm sorry.'

'Where, then? Where can she be? Where would she have gone?'

'We did the best we could.'

'Yes. I don't want you to think I'm not grateful.'

Celia tugged at John's sleeve again. 'Didn't they tell you where you're going? What about an address? You'll be miles away. How shall I get used to it?'

Edwin left Tony's side. He walked across to John.

'Did you hear? She wasn't on the bus.'

'I . . . heard.'

'I'm afraid it's time . . . it's nine-fifteen. You must go.'

Everybody was looking at John. He wondered what they expected of him. It seemed as if suddenly all the people in that room who for the past hour had been running about to comfort him were suddenly looking to him for reassurance. It was the last thing he felt he could give them. He wanted to raise his head and howl like a dog. He wanted to cry out for Margaret. He wanted to refuse to go. He wanted to tell them all that he didn't want to go to war. But he could not. That was not what they were all waiting for. That was not the stuff of which heroes were made. With a superhuman effort John conjured up a smile.

'Thank you all,' he said, 'for trying. It can't be helped. I . . . I shall just have to write to her, won't I'

He stood up and shouldered his kit. They all stood back for him. As steadily as he could John Porter walked towards the door.

CHAPTER SIX

Christmas that year was rather a subdued festival at the Ashton's. Not however on account of any shortages. Food wasn't going to be rationed until the New Year and Jean was able to put on her usual lavish spread for Christmas dinner. They were a large party and the dining-table had to be extended to its fullest length. David was home on leave and Robert back from school and as well as the family and Sefton and Tony who always came round Jean had invited Celia and Harry Porter. Otherwise, as Margaret would in any case have wanted to spend the day with her own family, they would have been on their own.

So the only person missing was John. He was in France doing, it seemed, nothing very much except write long letters home and practise his French on the locals. There was, as he kept telling Margaret, really no need to worry about him. But Margaret did worry. As she bustled about attending to everything Jean could not help but notice the pallor of Margaret's face and the shadows under her eyes. And whenever Jean managed to get everybody to forget the war and talk agreeably about other things Edwin would switch on the radio and shush them all to listen to yet another news bulletin.

This was not Christmas as Jean had always known it. She remembered other days when the children had been young and the house had been filled with laughter. Now none of her family were children any more and they were, Jean thought sadly, quickly losing those few vestiges of childhood's carefreeness and innocence that they still retained. Freda and Robert were far more grown up than David had been at their age. The war was putting old heads on young shoulders.

In January Philip got his call up papers. He left his job as a translator with no regrets. He had quite enjoyed it but never regarded it as more than a stop gap. Tony took him to the station on the day he left. Tony was eager to help anyone in uniform these days. Jean could see that he was restless and wondered how long it would be before he joined up. When he did, Sefton would be on his own in his big house with only the housekeeper for company.

Jean wanted to tell Tony not to do anything silly, but she could never find the right moment. It seemed to her that all the young people around her were driven by compulsions that she did not understand: David wrote with pleasure about the missions he had been on, Robert pined to be old enough to go to sea; Philip had gone gaily off into the army. Even Freda complained that she wished she was doing something more worthwhile than working in a hotel. All Jean wanted was to keep them safely at home, but she did not say so.

It was, therefore, a great comfort to her when Margaret came back home to live. Harry Porter brought her round unexpectedly one evening in the early spring.

'Would it be all right for Margaret to stay here for a bit?' he asked.

'All right. It's lovely,' said Jean. 'But why? Is anything the matter, Margaret?'

'No. I'm all right ... Don't fuss, please, Mum.'

'Then why ...?'

'For a rest,' said Harry. 'It'll do her good to be with you. Now that she's stopped work she's on her own a lot at our house ... well, of course, there's Celia, but a girl needs her own mother at a time like this.'

'I see,' said Jean.

Margaret explained a little more when they were on their own.

'She fussed me so. I had no peace. Oh, Mother, you've no idea how that woman goes on. All about John and the baby, and how much they mean to her. I can't stand too much of it. Anybody would think I didn't care about them at all. And I do. Oh, I do.'

'Yes. We all know you do.' Jean was concerned to soothe Margaret, who looked tenser and tireder than she ought to be. 'Perhaps you'll see John soon. He might get leave. There doesn't seem to be much happening over there, does there, really? And in any case you'll certainly see him when the baby's born. He'll get compassionate leave then.'

'But that's not till the end of the summer, Mother. That's a long time. Something will happen before then. I know it will.'

'Of course it will,' said Jean. 'The way they're talking John might be back home for good by then. Let's hope so.'

Margaret smiled but the frown crease did not fade from her forehead. 'I wish I could do something. Instead of just sitting around here getting fatter.'

'You're doing fine.' Jean patted Margaret's swelling tummy. 'You're doing what a whole army of men couldn't do no matter how hard they tried. And if you want to do a bit more, love, I've a pile of sheets here that need turning.'

Sheila started work at the N.A.A.F.I. Club. She called round one afternoon to tell Margaret and Jean about it.

'I started last Monday. I'm on the day-shift. The children go to my mother's after school. They like that. She spoils them a bit, I suppose, but I'm back for them before six. The hours aren't bad really. And then, there's the money.'

'It's all right, dear,' said Jean. 'I think you've done the right thing. I know David doesn't get paid very much and when he's late sending it ... Anyway, it's something to occupy your mind. We all need that, these days.'

'There's not that much to do,' said Sheila. 'We're not very busy. Really, from what's going on, you'd hardly know there was a war on.'

It was the lull before the storm. Because people's worst fears hadn't been realised they began to forget them. As spring established its hold even Margaret began to feel happy. Each afternoon she went for a walk in the park, sometimes on her own and sometimes with Jean, and watched as the buds on the trees swelled and the flowers, first the crocuses and primulas and then the daffodils and tulips, bloomed. Her baby was kicking now; she described the feeling to John in her letters to him.

John wrote back with absolute regularity and at great length. He told her as much as he could about what things were like in France and about what he did each day, but most of all he wrote about the baby and about the future. 'I'm saving up,' he wrote, 'I keep nearly all of my pay. No wine, women and song for me, you can be sure of that, Margaret. Then when I come back we might have enough to put down on a house. I'd like a new one, right on the edge of town so that we can easily take little John out into the country. We'll get him used to walking as soon as he's out of his pram. Have you got a pram yet? Write and tell me what it looks like as soon as you do.'

Margaret kept all John's letters in a box by the side of her bed, the same box she had kept her toys in as a child, Jean joked about them.

'If he goes on like this,' she said, 'you'll need a suitcase to keep them in. And after that a trunk. And after that a ...'

'Oh, Mum,' said Margaret, 'I hope not. I hope John'll be back home before it gets to that.'

Then quite suddenly, in the middle of May, the flow of letters ceased. There wasn't one for three days, then for four, then for a week. Margaret became silent and pale and hovered near the radio whenever there was a news bulletin.

The news was bad. The Germans invaded Holland and Belgium, then they moved into France. It was nearly summer and the bluebells were out and the roses were beginning to bud but Margaret gave up walking in the park.

Instead she spent the afternoons up in her bedroom writing

a letter to John. It grew to twenty pages long because she had nowhere to send it. There was not much that Jean could do except try and keep her anxiety to herself. She said reassuring things to Margaret, but they sounded hollow even in her own ears.

Jean and Margaret switched on the radio now as often as Edwin did. They listened to the bulletins in silence, not able to meet each other's eyes. Hungry for news Margaret pestered her father when he came in from work.

'Dad, have you heard anything? Isn't there anybody who knows what's really happening?'

'They say the lads are coming back,' Edwin said. 'The army's being evacuated from Dunkirk.'

'Who is? What units? Where are they coming to?' Margaret demanded.

'The chap I spoke to didn't know,' said Edwin. 'It sounds to be a bit of a shambles. But at least they're coming back. Try not to worry, love. You might get John back quicker than you expected after all.'

'Like this?' said Margaret. 'This isn't how I wanted him back. Still, so long as he comes . . . don't you know anything more, Dad?'

Sheila was moved from the N.A.A.F.I. Club to an emergency canteen. There were only four of them on the staff there and they hardly had time to set out what little equipment they had been supplied with before the first of the repatriated soldiers arrived. Sheila was horrified by the state they were in and by the tales they had to tell. She was run off her feet and worked sixteen hours a day; she had to let the children sleep at her mother's. But she didn't mind. She was glad to do what she could to help the men. Most of them were young and all of them were very tired. A situation of stability had been turned into one of retreat so suddenly that they were bewildered. Sheila tried to find out from some of them exactly what had happened, for Margaret's sake.

'How did you get across?' she asked, 'Do you think there were many left behind? Only, my sister-in-law's husband's out there.'

Some of the men talked compulsively; a little red-headed private from Birmingham who looked scarcely any older than

Robert Ashton held on to Sheila's sleeve when she had put his cup of tea down and told her how he had waited in the sea for a boat to pick him up.

'I had this mate, see,' he said. 'I'd been with him all along. He had this fur coat with him. He'd rescued it, he said, for his wife, and he walked bloody miles carrying it. Only he couldn't swim, see? He'd walked well enough but he couldn't swim, so it was no use, all that walking. We were in the sea and I held him up, but my arm went kind of numb. You know how you go, numb. I couldn't grip. So he went down. The coat went first, and then him. And then the bleeding boat came. Only it was too late. He was down. Right on the bloody bottom.' Sheila didn't after all, tell Margaret what she had heard.

Eventually the flow of men slackened and Sheila had time to relax a little. And to think. She had something to think about. One morning, at the height of the rush, she had gone home to find a letter on the doormat; a letter with the same postmark that David's always had. But this letter was not from David. Indeed, Sheila didn't know who it was from but she wished she'd never received it. Because the letter had talked about David and a girl. A girl, the letter said, whose name was Peggy. A girl who was expecting David's baby.

Sheila tried to forget about it. She told herself that it couldn't possibly be true. But she wasn't sure, and until David got leave and she was able to talk about it face to face with him she couldn't be sure. Sheila was beginning to realise how easily that kind of thing could happen. She saw it going on around her at the canteen. Mrs Ironside, the woman she worked with, was quite open about the fact that she took her fun where she could find it. Sheila wasn't shocked at Mrs Ironside. She had not led a sheltered life. But for herself she wasn't interested.

Even so, she knew that she was pleased and flattered by the attention of the canteen's driver, Bob O'Connell. She was lonely. David got leave infrequently and she never knew when to expect him. It was nice to have a man who admired her She realised that if she gave him only the slightest encouragement Bob's attention wouldn't stop at just giving her lifts in the truck. And if it would be so easy for her it would be even easier for David. So try as she might Sheila couldn't forget what she had been told about David and Peggy.

On the second Sunday in June Margaret and Jean went to church together. It was a special service, a thanksgiving for the men who had come back from Dunkirk. The weather was beautiful, it was a perfect English June day, and the congregation sang the hymns with gusto. Jean listened to Margaret's clear voice pealing out next to her and looked at Margaret's dry eyes and wondered where her daughter got her courage from. Margaret had nothing to be thankful for. There was still no news of John, but she was carrying on bravely.

Too bravely, Jean sometimes thought. She worried about the feelings that Margaret was penning up. If, when news did come, it was the worst news, would Margaret pay the price for her courage and break down? And if she did, would it be bad for the boy? There was nothing to do, Jean decided, but emulate Margaret and hope only for the best.

After Church Margaret said: 'I think I should go round and see John's parents this afternoon.'

'Should you, dear,' Jean asked. 'Are you sure you're feeling up to it? You don't want to tire yourself.'

'I'm all right,' said Margaret. 'It's over two months before the baby yet, I'll get tireder than this before the end. I think I should go. It's . . . it can't be easy for them either, can it?'

Harry Porter opened the door for her when she arrived at the house in Egerton Street. He led the way into the empty, stuffy front room. The sight of it oppressed Margaret. It reminded her of the many unhappy evenings that she had spent here with Celia.

'Where's . . .' asked Margaret. She had never found a name to call her mother-in-law. It seemed quite inappropriate to call her either mother or Celia and to say Mrs Porter seemed too obviously to point out the estrangement between them.

'She's upstairs,' said Harry. 'She's gone to bed with one of her headaches. You know how it is.'

'I know. Are you . . . managing?'

'We have to, don't we? I've joined the L.D.V., did you know? Only I can't get down there very often, not with Celia as she is. She's taking it very hard. I try and keep busy, though. I've been trying to mend John's old radio, the two valve set he made when he was a boy. Before you knew him. I thought it might come in for the shelter. But I can't get it to go. It needs John . . .'

'Let's put the kettle on.' Margaret looked at Harry with concern and led the way into the kitchen. 'You look as if you could do with a drink. You need somebody to look after you.'

'Yes. Well, I manage as best I can.' Harry stood back as Margaret got out some cups. 'Celia's not been at all well. You mustn't blame her. She used to be different when John was little. And he loves her, so there must be something . . .'

'Yes. I'm sorry. I wish I could . . . I wish I could do more to help.'

'Now, Margaret. You come when you can. It means a lot to me, seeing you, but you must think of yourself, not of me. You've got enough to bear.'

Margaret pressed her fingers hard against her eyes. 'I went to the station, did I tell you? I shouldn't have done, but I couldn't just keep sitting at home and waiting. I watched the trains coming in, I stood near the barrier and watched the faces of the men coming through . . . I thought I saw him at least three times.' She paused. 'I don't think I shall ever want to go on a station again, ever. I didn't tell them at home. I can only tell you. It helps me to talk to you. You . . . keep my courage up.'

'I do? I do?' Harry sounded incredulous. He had the heel of his hand against the edge of the gas stove to support himself but even so he seemed to sway. The steam from the kettle veiled him from Margaret but through it Margaret could see that his face was ashen. 'Perhaps we have to help each other,' she said. 'If we didn't have other people to lean on, what would we do? You look as if you need this cup of tea. At least that's something I can do for you.'

When Margaret had gone Harry stood at the bottom of the stairs for a moment listening for Celia. Then he went to the cupboard under the stairs and took out a bottle of whisky. The cupboard was small and dark and dusty. Normally it contained only the gas meter and a few left-over relics of John's childhood—a cricket bat, a deflated football and a box of unsorted stamps. As he reached into it Harry's hand was shaking. He was very conscious of the shame of what he was doing. To drink in secret seemed so cowardly and deceitful that it affronted all his ideas of what he was. Yet he could not help himself. It had taken all his strength to keep up a brave front for Margaret. He must replenish it before he had to do the same for

Celia. 'Dutch courage,' thought Harry, as he drank his whisky. 'It's better than nothing.' He felt quite alone and inadequate. At a time like this he must seek courage where he could.

Celia came down soon afterwards. She walked into the room with that peculiar, stiff gait that she had adopted more and more since John had gone away. She was like a sleepwalker except that underneath her smooth façade her brain ticked away relentlessly and, as it seemed to Harry, malevolently. She used her pain, he thought, to hurt him, and he flinched before she even spoke.

'You think I don't know you've been drinking, don't you?' she said. 'Hiding it in the meter cupboard. Well, as far as I'm concerned just go ahead ... drink the whole bottle ... drink yourself to death if you must.'

'Celia, don't.' Harry looked at his wife and wondered how he could get through to her. Her face was stiff and expressionless, hiding the feelings that gave vent to her lancing words. Harry felt that she was a long long way from him, retreating down a dark tunnel.

'I'm not a drinking man normally,' he said. 'Only now ... I was trying to spare your feelings.'

'You know what John thinks about drink. I know what John would say.'

Not that, thought Harry. If only Celia would help him instead of using his love for John as a weapon to hurt him. It shouldn't be like this. It hadn't always been. Harry made a last effort to reach his wife.

'Celia,' he said, 'Please don't. This is me, this is Harry ... I loved John, too. Do you remember that Spring before he was born. I took you to Southport and the beach was empty. You wore your fox fur. You weren't like this then. Celia, help me.'

But Celia had not listened, or she pretended not to hear. She carried on talking like an automaton, not even turning her head to look at him.

'When John comes back,' she said, 'I'll tell him. Let the Germans have France, I say, only send our boys back. He will come back, won't he? You said he would. You promised me he would, and you pride yourself on your promises, don't you, Harry? I cling to that.'

Harry watched his wife's mouth move as she talked but he couldn't bear to listen any more to what she was saying. He thought instead, with longing, of his hidden bottle. It was true what he had said, he wasn't a drinking man. But now he needed alcohol to dim his senses and blur his mind so that he couldn't hear Celia's desperate confidence or remember Margaret's brave hopes. Because Harry couldn't share those hopes and soon he must dash them. In his pocket was a telegram from the War Office.

It had been addressed to Margaret, but Harry had had no doubts about opening it. It had seemed to him much better that Margaret should know from him that John was missing and believed killed rather than from a piece of paper. What he had not allowed for was that his courage would fail him. Face to face with Margaret this afternoon he had not been able to speak. If only he could protect her for ever from knowing what he knew.

At length Celia stopped talking. She lay on the couch with her eyes closed; either her flow of words or the sedative pills she had taken had soothed her. But as soon as Harry stood up her eyes snapped open again.

'Are you going out? You can't think of leaving me.'

'No.' Harry sought for something to occupy her mind and his, something that would stop her talking. There was a book on the end of the settee. 'I'll read to you. Would you like that? I used to, do you remember? How about this?' He picked up the book and opened it where a slip of paper marked the place. He pushed his finger between the leaves near the back cover, separating out a wedge of pages at random. He would read that far. The feel of the thick paper reassured him. There must be hundreds, thousands of words there, and none of them referred to John. They would be his hour glass, giving him time. Not until they ran out did he need to think again of going to tell Margaret what he would rather she never knew.

Sheila was just finishing work at the canteen. She put her coat on wearily. It was too late now to go round to her mother's as she had planned to do. If she saw the children too late in the evening just before they went to bed it upset both them and her; the last time she had done so Peter had cried himself to sleep when she had gone. She contemplated visiting the Ashton's. She hated the thought of going back alone to her quiet, dark, unlived-in house.

Just as she picked up her bag Bob O'Connell came in.
'Going off?' he said.
'Yes.'
'So am I.'
'Oh,' said Sheila, and waited for what she knew Bob would say. She liked him very much. Since she had made it plain to him that she wasn't available for what Mrs Ironside called 'a bit of fun' they had become good friends. He was as lonely as Sheila. More so really, because his wife had left him and he had no family. Sheila felt sorry for him, and as well as that she admired the indomitable way he fetched and carried for the canteen in spite of his crippled leg. Whenever she was in danger of feeling sorry for herself a few words with Bob put her troubles into perspective again.
'Can I give you a lift?' he said.
'Thank you. I was hoping you'd ask.'
'You knew I would.'
'I must say you're very kind to me,' Sheila said.
'You know it's a pleasure to do anything for you.'
'Now, now,' said Sheila, laughing at him. 'Don't let's give Mrs Ironside food for thought. She has enough ideas without you saying things like that.'
As he drove along Bob told Sheila a little more about his wife. It was a new experience for Sheila to be confided in. Normally she was the person who sought advice, not the one who gave it. She had for so long needed support and comfort from Jean or Edwin that she found it flattering when Bob asked for opinions from her. Because Bob was older than she Sheila would have expected him to know all the answers. That he did not made her feel strong.
When he stopped the truck outside her house and switched the engine off it was suddenly quiet. Bob's face was peaky in the shaded cap. Sheila turned to thank him, and then said, on a sudden impulse:
'You wouldn't be hungry, would you?'
'No,' said Bob. 'I'm fine, thanks.' But he still stared at her and made no move to open her door.
'I don't believe you. You're being polite,' Sheila said.
'No . . . honestly . . .'
'Only I've hardly eaten a thing all day,' said Sheila. 'I've been that busy dishing up. And I've got a week's rations in

hand, nearly. I'm asking you. Don't be shy.'

'Well, then,' said Bob, 'If you put it like that.'

They were just finishing eating when David walked in. He had let himself in quietly through the back door and appeared quite suddenly from the scullery. In his blue uniform he looked big and handsome. Sheila saw him first, and could hardly believe her eyes.

'David,' she said, 'What are you doing here?' She got up to run to him. Then she saw him look at Bob and the frown on his face stopped her in her tracks before she reached his side. She stood between the two of them, looking from one to the other. Neither of them spoke and their silence began to be embarrassing. It was obviously up to Sheila to bridge the gap.

'David,' she said tentatively, 'this is Bob. At the canteen. He's brought me home. Bob, this is my husband. I didn't expect you, David.'

'So I see,' said David heavily.

Bob stood up awkwardly. He balanced on his sound leg trying to push his chair back under the table. 'I'd better be off,' he said. Sheila suddenly felt furious. David was glowering at Bob fiercely. It was obvious what he was thinking. Sheila remembered the letter that was in her handbag. How dared David think that she ... 'Don't go,' she said to Bob. 'There's no need.'

'Oh, I think so,' began Bob.

'There seems no point in staying now,' said David. Sheila clenched her hands to prevent herself speaking out. It would be better if she said nothing. What she had to say to David she must say when they were on their own. She could apologise to Bob another day. She helped Bob with his coat, smiling as nicely as she could.

'Thanks very much for the lift. It's such a help. See you tomorrow, eh?'

'Thank you,' said Bob. 'Er ... I hope ...' He held out his hand to David. 'Nice to have met you.'

'Mmm,' said David. He held open the scullery door pointedly. 'Coming out through here?'

When Bob had gone David walked to the armchair and sat down. Sheila watched him in silence. David stretched his feet towards the empty grate. 'Home sweet home,' he said.

'What do you mean by that?'

'What do you think I mean? I come home to see my wife and kids and what do I find? An empty house. No wife, no kids. I've been half-way round Liverpool looking for you.'

'How can I be in when I don't know you're coming?' Sheila said. 'Am I supposed to sit here all on my own, no money, no company, week after week, just on the off chance that you'll decide to turn up. What do you think I am?'

'My wife, that's what I think you are. And I think your place is here, looking after my kids. Where are they? What have you done with them?'

'They're at my mother's of course. Couldn't you have thought of that?'

'Why should I think of it? That isn't where they should be. Their place is here, and so is yours.'

'Is it?' Sheila was furious now. 'Whose fault is it then that I need to go out to work? Whose fault is it then that I had no money? At least they've got clothes now, and enough to eat. It was more than we were likely to have when we all depended on you. And I want the company. What company are you when you're miles away?'

David gestured in the direction of the back door. 'Is he what you call company? Is he what you go out to work for?'

'He's a friend, that's all.' Sheila was shouting now. 'He's never even been inside this house before today.'

'I see.' David was deliberately offensive. 'Got here in the nick of time, did I?'

Sheila was in tears. 'What do you mean by that? How dare you talk to me like that,' she said.

'I come home to my wife and what do I find? A cosy little tea party going on.'

'Yes, and that's all. Just a friendly meal, no more. We're not all like you.'

'What do you mean by that?' David was flushed and now he leaned forward in his chair. Sheila was glad that at last her anger had touched him.

'Well,' said Sheila, playing her trump card. 'Do you know a girl called Peggy?'

David turned his head away sharply, and said nothing. For the first time Sheila began to be really frightened. She had supposed there was a certain amount of truth in the letter, but not much. No doubt there was a Peggy. Perhaps, even, David had been out with her. He had always had an eye for the girls. That was how she had got him. But until now she had not cared to think there might be more to it than that. Surely it couldn't all be true. Not about the baby. Sheila's heart beat so that she could hardly breathe. David's silence seemed like an admission. Sheila wished she had never heard about Peggy, but now that she had it seemed imperative to know the truth.

'Tell me, David,' she said, almost pleading.

'Say again,' he said, his voice muffled. 'What's her name?'

'Peggy,' said Sheila softly, eager to keep his words flowing.

'Where've you got that from?'

'I had a letter. It said ... it said she's pregnant.'

'It's some crank.' David was suddenly vehement. 'Some girl ... I don't know. I meet them, of course. But I give them the brush off. I'm a married fellow, aren't I? Perhaps one of them turned nasty and wrote to you.'

Sheila wanted to be convinced, but she was not.

'I don't think it's from a girl,' she said. 'I think it's from a man.'

'How do you work that out?'

'I just think it is. It just seems like a man. The writing ... and it's more ... dignified than a girl would write.'

'All right,' said David, turning round now to face Sheila and talking with emphasis as if he must compel her to believe him. 'So this judy fancies me, so this chap that fancies her gets all worked up. He gets my address from the Records and he writes a letter. To cause trouble. You don't want that, do you, Sheila?'

'Oh, David ...' Sheila tried to believe him. She thought more of David than he did of her, she had known that from the beginning. For nine years she had forgiven all his faults, because, with all those faults he was the one man she wanted. Because of that she had put up with his unreliability and extravagance and she was willing to go on doing so. But this accusation, if it were true, would be too much. She could not bear the thought that David might love another woman. She stared into his face and he looked back up at her, guileless, a smile on his lips. 'Come on, Sheila,' he said coaxingly, and held his hand out to her. 'I've only got a couple of hours.'

She went to her handbag. From it she took the letter. She held it out to him. 'Here it is. You'd better explain it.'

'Why?' He was still looking at her steadfastly. 'Throw it away, Sheila,' he said. His face was flushed from looking in the fire and his smile was uncertain. He looked, thought Sheila, just like Peter looked when he asked her for something that he thought she would not be able to give. The comparison melted all her resolution. She tore the letter up and threw it into the grate. David took some matches from his pocket. Kneeling on the hearthrug, he set light to the pieces.

'There,' he said, turning to run his hands up Sheila's calves. 'That's that. And I've still got another couple of hours.'

'I think I'd better get back to the canteen,' said Sheila, wanting to pay him back for the anxiety he had caused her. 'I sleep on a camp-bed there when we're busy, you know.'

'Now,' said David, running his hands higher. 'This is your husband that's come home, don't you know that?'

'And there's the washing up to do,' said Sheila, teasing.

David stood up and put his arms round Sheila. 'We can do that after,' he said.

'After what?'

David bent his head to kiss her. She felt the familiar surge of excitement that she always felt when David wanted her. Already the thought of Peggy which had loomed so large all week, was beginning to fade. She didn't want the story to be true. Surely it could not be true. David was here and for the moment at least she was happy that he was. That was enough to be going on with.

CHAPTER SEVEN

When at last Harry steeled himself to carry his news to Margaret she seemed to take it better than anybody could have expected. Her hand was steady as she held it out for the crumpled telegram and her eyes were dry as she read what it said. 'The War Office regrets . . .' she said in a thin, high, bewildered voice. She handed the telegram to her father.

'Missing . . .' read Edwin. 'Believed killed. Margaret, love . . .'

'Missing,' said Margaret, still in that high, disembodied voice. 'You see, they just don't know where he is. He could be anywhere . . . a prisoner of war. It'd take a bit of time to hear about that, wouldn't it?'

Edwin looked from his daughter to his wife and then to Harry Porter. None of them could meet his gaze, and no one spoke. Margaret's calm was brittle. It might shatter at one wrong word, and none of them wanted to risk saying that word. Jean, with an obvious effort, pulled herself together first.

'Tea?' she said. 'Mr Porter, I'm sure you'd like a cup.'

'I don't know,' said Harry. 'I shouldn't leave Celia too long. She's asleep . . . tablets from the doctor. I don't know . . .'

'I would,' said Margaret, stronger at that moment than any of them. 'A cup of tea is just what we all need. I'll go and put the kettle on.'

In the days that followed, when she wept for John, she did so in private. In front of the family her self-control was rigid. So rigid that it worried Jean. She would have liked it if Margaret could have cried on her shoulder as she had when she was a child over much smaller misfortunes. Jean had been able to comfort those childish woes but this older Margaret seemed to deny the need for her mother's comfort.

But she betrayed the strain she was under by other means than tears. She started to carry her gas mask everywhere she went; she wept for the ruin of the garden when it was dug up for the Anderson shelter, and she turned on Sefton when he complained when Tony deserted the business to go into the Navy. Jean was glad when Margaret showed emotion. Even anger or sorrow seemed better than the hard calm with which Margaret otherwise faced the world.

As the summer wore on Jean's distress grew. It wasn't the big things that bothered her, the news from abroad and the threat of invasion so much as the petty restrictions of everyday life: the rationing, the queues that were beginning to form everywhere, the eerie silence on Sunday mornings when no familiar church bells rang.

But she kept her feelings to herself, and the rest of the family did not seem to share them. Indeed Freda, and Philip when he came home on leave after his unit had been withdrawn from the Channel Isles at the end of June seemed positively exhilarated by the desperateness of the country's situation. 'We're better off without allies,' they declared. 'Now we're on our own at least we've only ourselves to worry about.'

Edwin too seemed to find the challenge stimulating. With

Tony gone, all the responsibility for the works was on his shoulders. His task was not made any easier by the fact that both men and paper were in short supply, but although he was working hard and for long hours he never seemed too tired to be patient and cheerful in front of Margaret.

David, too, seemed happy. When he came home on leave he was jauntier, more self-confident than he had used to be. He was going out on bombing missions over Germany regularly and although he didn't talk about it much at home and when he did he made light of it, Jean worried about him too. It seemed to her that through the long, hot days of that exceptional summer she was leading a double life, cultivating a false face with which to face the world and hiding behind it all her anxiety and distress. She wondered sometimes if other people were doing the same, if all the women she met in the queue at the butcher's and all those men who, like Harry Porter, turned out to parade for the Home Guard in the evenings after a hard day's work really felt as steadfast and confident as they looked.

Margaret's baby was due at the beginning of September. During the summer Margaret and Jean between them made or managed to buy most of the things that it would need. It was about the only thing that Margaret could be made to take an interest in.

One afternoon she and her mother went on what Margaret called a 'rooting-out expedition' to the boxroom at the top of the house. There, from underneath a pile of old carpet and a box of unmatched crockery Jean unearthed the cot and the bath that had been stored there since Robert had grown out of them.

'Lovely,' said Margaret, rubbing at the dust on the cot with the corner of her skirt. 'Just get Dad going on this with a pot of paint and it'll be as good as new.'

'Yes.' Jean sat back on her heels and surveyed the piles of outgrown or outworn objects massed around her. 'I don't know, I seem to have been up here more often in these last twelve months than I was in twelve years before that. What with toys for the evacuees and old pans for Spitfires...I never thought so much of this would come in useful again.'

'This is your moment of triumph,' said Margaret. 'This is when you can get back at Dad and the boys for teasing you about the way you hoard things. Who knows, before we've finished every single thing in here will have come in useful.'

'Oh, Margaret, not everything.' Jean laughed. 'Some of these things have been here a very long time. That umbrella stand over there was your grandmother's. I can't see a use for that, even in a war. Though I suppose that when I put most of these things up here I never thought I'd want them again.'

'You see,' said Margaret, 'it's an ill wind . . . ' She stopped, and Jean saw her face flush. The room was dark and intimate. Jean took her opportunity.

'Margaret,' she said, 'you do know, don't you, that you'll always have your father and me? I don't say much about it because . . . I suppose it's easier not. But I want you to remember that we'll always do our best to look after you.'

'You're doing very well.' Margaret's voice was muffled. 'I don't know what I'd do without you with John . . . away. You and Dad and . . . hope are what keep me going.'

'Hope and courage,' said Jean. 'That's what you've got. And the baby. That'll help. You won't have long to wait for that, now.'

The following week, on the 18th of August 1940, air raids began over Liverpool. The Ashtons were as prepared as they could be. Jean had stored the family documents and as many other things as she could persuade Edwin to allow her the space for in the cupboard under the stairs and Philip had made the shelter in the garden as cosy as possible. But despite these preparations the wavering whine of the siren heralded uncomfortable and fearful nights.

The Anderson shelter in the garden was damp and dark and sour-smelling. The wooden bunks that Edwin installed in it were hard and it was very cramped. After two sleepless nights Margaret refused to go into it any more.

'I'll take my chance in the house,' she said, 'I can go under the table when the planes come close. With the baby so near and me so big I just feel too . . . oppressed in there.' After looking at her pale strained face Jean, anxious though she was to have her family where they would be safest, didn't insist.

One evening at the end of the month just as the family were contemplating having an early night with a view to catching up on some lost sleep, there was a knock on the door.

'Who's that?' Freda wondered. 'Might it be David? He's on

leave, isn't he?'

'It's all right, I'll go,' said Edwin. 'I don't like you girls opening the door when it's getting dark.'

'Why ever not?' asked Freda, teasing him. 'Do you think it might be a German parachutist wanting to ask the way to Buckingham Palace? You don't believe those tales they tell, do you?'

'Of course not. Some people are a lot of silly scaremongers. Even so, I'm the man of the house and I'll go.'

'Of course, it might be the stork,' said Freda to Margaret. 'Where you expecting it tonight?'

'I hope not,' said Margaret. 'Not for another four days. And in daylight, if I can manage it. About teatime, I think. Would that be convenient for you all?'

Edwin came back pushing a small, dirty boy in front of him.

'This is our caller,' he said. 'Not quite what we expected, is it?'

Margaret was touched by the air of combined bravado and bewilderment on the boy's face. She got up heavily and went to him.

'What's your name?'

A big man in a policeman's uniform came in behind Edwin. It was Jack Sanderson, a neighbour from across the back.

'Alfred,' he said. 'This is Alfred Powner.'

'Come in, Jack,' said Jean. 'Is this an official visit?'

'Well, yes and no.' Jack took off his helmet and smoothed his hair. 'This lad's been found wandering on Lime Street station. He's come from Sheffield, he says, and he's been evacuated.'

'Evacuated to Liverpool?' Freda was incredulous. 'It doesn't make sense.'

'That's what he says.'

'Oh, anything can happen,' said Margaret. 'Some of the kids from school ended up near Manchester.'

'Anyway,' Jack said, 'I thought I'd just take him to our house for the night. Just until we can get in touch with Sheffield in the morning. But now Mary's in bed with her back and can't cope and ... well, she suggested you. I hope it's all right.'

'Of course it's all right.' Jean was brisk. 'We've always room for boys here. I should have, with my own away. He can go in the attic. It'll be no trouble. You'll be all right with us, Alfred.'

'Right.' Jack let out a breath of relief. 'Thank goodness for that. I'll be round in the morning, then. Thank you very much, Jean.'

While Jean went to get the room ready Margaret took Alfred under her wing, making him wash and encouraging him to eat. Not that he needed much encouragement. Watching the boy wolf the food that Margaret had provided out of the Ashtons' depleted larder Edwin wondered about his background. The child was dirty and his clothes were very poor; he had the hunted, wary look that Edwin had noticed was characteristic of the children who lived in the warrenous streets near Sheila and David or in the tenements he passed on his way to work every day. He looked a neglected child, thought Edwin, and unhappy, and he was probably not very trustworthy. But his coming would be a blessing if it provided Margaret with an interest and an outlet for the feelings of tenderness that she had bottled up so long and so dangerously.

Alfred did provide an outlet of a sort for Margaret's feelings, but not in quite the way that Edwin had had in mind. As she was tucking him up in bed the boy said to her: 'You're going to have a baby, aren't you, Miss? Your belly's fat.'

'Well,' said Margaret, taken aback by his bluntness. 'Yes, as a matter of fact, I am.'

'Are you having a boy or a girl?'

'I'm taking pot luck, like everybody else.'

' 'Ave you got a chap?' asked Alfred inexorably.

'Yes. I've got a chap.'

'Is he in the Navy?'

'He's . . . he was a soldier.'

'Is he dead?'

'Dead' repeated Margaret. That was a word nobody had used in that house for three long months. Edwin and Jean and Freda skirted round it as if it were an unexploded bomb. So it fell from Alfred's lips raw and fresh. a word new minted with its meaning nor blurred by use.

'Killed by a Jerry!' insisted Alfred, with calm interest and the callousness of a child already scarred by war. 'Did a Jerry stick a bayonet in him? Where is he now?'

For the first time in months Margaret's tears flowed freely.

She was on her bed when the siren went and the noise of her grief drowned its wailing. It wasn't until Freda had banged on her door three times that she recovered herself enough to go downstairs to where the family were preparing for another long night's vigil.

Philip had come in after an evening with friends just as the siren went. He was home on leave and was wearing his uniform. Margaret noticed with some relief when she came down that Philip had usurped her place in Alfred's attentions. It was Philip now that Alfred was questioning with bloodthirsty intensity.

'Have you killed Jerries?'

'No,' said Philip.

'Why not?' Philip looked taken aback. Margaret was glad to see that he didn't find it any easier to deal with Alfred's directness than she had done.

'Because I haven't seen any to kill,' said Philip at last.

'Would you if you did?' Alfred persisted.

'I'd have to, wouldn't I?'

'Why?'

'Because if I didn't they'd kill me.'

Alfred's hard composure melted quite suddenly. He was like a boy who had climbed too high a tree to frighten his mother only to find when he got to the top that he was frightened too. He huddled himself into the corner of the settee, a lost child.

'I don't like being at war,' he said.

'Neither do I,' said Philip. As Alfred's confidence wavered Philip's grew firmer; this was more the situation he expected. 'Keep this to yourself,' he said, 'but I don't think we're supposed to.'

'Do the Jerries?' Alfred asked.

'Shouldn't think so.'

'Then why are we at war?'

Philip surveyed the child at his side with a mixture of amusement and respect.

'You ask some pretty tough questions, Alfred, do you know that?'

'Why?' said Alfred.

Jean came in at this point with the teapot.

'Here we are,' she said, 'the cup that cheers. Britain's secret weapon. Only go easy on the sugar. There's some saccharine tablets here.'

While she was pouring out, Edwin organised his family.

'The minute we hear anything,' he said, 'I want you four ... that's Margaret, Freda, this lad here and you Jean to get under the stairs. The shelter's flooded, we can't use it tonight.'

'What about you and Philip?' Jean asked.

'We'll go under the table.'

'It's a very nice glory hole under the stairs,' Freda said. 'But there's only room for two in a standing position, I'd say. Breathing in turns. Looking at our Margaret ...'

'All right, all right,' said Margaret. 'No need to be personal. I'll go under the table.'

'Me too,' said Alfred.

'Stay with me,' said Margaret. 'We'll be all right.'

Everyone fell silent, listening. The raiders had drawn near. The throbbing sound of a bomber's engines penetrated the blacked-out windows and the closed doors, making the cosy room seem suddenly exposed. Margaret tried not to listen, and wracked her brain for something to say. It was better to talk, to ignore the noise, but none the less she could not help herself. The family sat silent for long, horrible minutes, gauging the plane's trajectory, hypnotised by the noise, and by the fear of what was to come.

It was Alfred who caused the diversion. There was a yell and a crash and his cup of tea landed on the floor.

'Oh.' Jean leapt up. 'Alfred, Alfred, my carpet.'

Alfred cowered away, his hand to his face. Jean looked at him more gently.

'Don't worry, it'll dry.'

'She won't hit you,' said Margaret, concerned for his fear.

'Worse things happen at sea,' said Jean. 'I'll get a cloth.'

Alfred watched her mop up. 'I've never seen the sea,' he said. 'Where is it?'

'Never seen it,' said Jean. 'Well, Philip must take you. In the morning, after ... all this ... he'll take you down to the ferry. You can see it from there. There's the estuary and then the sea. It's not far.'

'Can you walk it?'

'Well, to the river you could.'

The noise of the bombers was louder now, and from somewhere not very far away came the fearful whistle and the crunch of a falling bomb. All the family flinched. They were familiar by now with the banshee wail and the shuddering crash of the bombs, but familiarity had not brought contempt. Each evening the first bomb that fell seemed destined for them, every time the house shook Jean wondered if the next time it would fall and crush them all.

'Right,' said Edwin authoritatively. He looked at his watch like a man who has been waiting for a long time and at last hears his train come in. 'Lights out, I think, Freda. Let's get ourselves sorted out.'

Margaret, with some difficulty, crawled under the table. Jean had provided blankets to keep them warm, but no matter how Margaret lay her back ached.

'Anybody got a spare cushion?' she asked.

'What?' said Philip. 'You've already got more than your ration. How many have you got?'

'There's more of me than there is of you.'

'Have mine, love,' said Edwin. 'Philip, remember how Margaret is.'

'Sorry,' said Philip.

'What a time to choose to be like this,' said Margaret. 'Still, I didn't exactly choose, did I?'

'Do you feel all right?' asked Edwin.

'I'm fine. It's just this backache.'

'Should I go and get your mother?'

'Oh no, no need for that.'

But as Margaret lay there, trying to be brave, shifting her feet when Philip and her father crawled out during a lull in the raid to have a quick smoke, she began to be less and less certain that there was no need to call her mother. Her backache grew into a girdle of pain; she remembered what she had been told and tried to time its fluctuations, counting the seconds as exactly as she could except when an extra loud shriek or crash from the rage outside made her forget where she was up to. At last she felt she must do something.

'Dad. Are you awake?'

'Yes. How could I sleep with you lying there shifting about and grunting.'

'Was I? I'm sorry, I didn't know.'

'Don't worry, it's not you kept me awake as much as that lot outside. What is it, Margaret.'

'Well, I'm sorry about this, but I think something's happening. The baby, I mean.'

'Well, well.' Edwin pushed the blanket off his knees and prodded Philip's shoulder. 'I'll go and get your mother and Philip can phone up. Seems we've got something to thank Jerry for, after all. If it wasn't for him I'd have to get out of my warm bed in the middle of the night, and I wouldn't care for that, at all.'

For a little while everything was bustle. Jean came with hot-water bottles and rubbed Margaret's back, Edwin lit candles. The electricity was off, and with it the phone; Philip was despatched through the screaming night to see if he could find a doctor. Margaret was beginning to be frightened as her pains grew more and more severe. 'Don't let him go out,' she said. 'If something happens . . .'

'Nothing will,' said Philip. 'If it's going to get me it'll get me wherever . . . anyway, I could do with a breath of fresh air. I'll be as quick as I can.'

'Lie as quiet as you can,' said Jean. 'Someone'll come soon.'

'Mum, I want to tell you . . .'

'Yes,' said Jean, encouragingly.

Something about this night, after the sleeplessness of so many others, something about Alfred's directness and the pain she was in had crumbled Margaret's defences. She wanted to cross the sheltering no man's land that she formed around herself, she wanted to confide in her mother and accept Jean's help in return.

'It's about John,' Margaret said, 'that letter I had the other day. I was going to keep it to myself . . . as if by not talking about it I could make it not real. But now . . . it wasn't just a form, like I said. The army had sent it . . . it'd been found . . . it was a photograph of me that John had. He'd written on the back "All I care about is you and the boy." He was sure it would be a boy. Somebody found his pay book, you see.'

'Oh, Margaret . . .'

'But not his tab. They haven't found his tab. So he's still missing, you see. Nothing's final.'

'You know what Mr Porter told you,' said Jean, not believing what she said. 'About if he'd been made a prisoner and how long it might take . . . it's all such a muddle,' he said.

'You mean I should still hope?' Margaret asked.
'Yes, I think you should.'
'But what shall I do when I stop hoping?'

Philip came back just as the All Clear sounded.
'Ambulance on its way,' he said.
'You've been a long time,' said Jean. 'We were beginning to wonder . . . where you'd got to.'
'Doctor Miles was out, and so was his wife. I found a warden's post and they got through to the hospital for me.'
His voice woke Freda out of her doze in the chair.
'What time is it?' she asked sleepily.
'Twenty past four,' said Edwin. 'The All Clear's gone.'
'Oooh.' Freda groaned and put her hand up to her head. 'I ache.'
'Come on.' Edwin took her elbow and urged her to her feet. 'Up the wooden hill to Bedfordshire.'
'Leave me alone,' Freda moaned.
'You've got to be up for work in three hours, chick,' said Edwin. 'Come on, I'll help you up the stairs.'
Jean surveyed the untidy room and started to collect the dirty teacups. 'Well,' she said, 'that's another night we've got through. Philip, go upstairs and get Margaret's case down. And tell Alfred . . . where is Alfred?'
They all stood peering round, as if the boy might be hidden behind a chair or under the carpet.
'He's not here,' said Philip. 'I'll go and look under the stairs.'
'And shout up to your father to look round the beds.'
'I haven't seen him since Philip went out,' said Margaret. 'Did he go out with you?'
'No,' said Philip. 'Not that I know of. I wouldn't have taken him.'
'Look everywhere,' said Jean. 'Quickly. He must be somewhere.'
But the boy could not be found. The search was still going on when the ambulance came.
'What will you do if he doesn't turn up?' asked Margaret, struggling into her coat.
'Don't worry about that.' Edwin picked up her suitcase and patted her shoulder. 'You just worry about yourself. I'll see to Alfred.'

The ambulance man was waiting in the doorway. 'Ready, lady.'

'Yes. I'm sorry to get you out on a night like this.'

'Don't worry. We were out already. A call like yours is a pleasure compared to some we've had, I can tell you.'

'Is it . . . bad?'

'Not too good.'

'I feel so awful.' Margaret gasped and steadied herself against the door jamb as the pain built up again. 'Having a baby . . . seems so . . . inappropriate . . . at a time like this.'

'Take your time.' The man waited until Margaret recovered herself. 'You'll be all right. If it wasn't for people like you where would we be after this lot?'

'After?' said Margaret. 'I hadn't thought of that. It seems impossible to think of things being different from this, to think of them being normal. I can't imagine that this will ever end.'

'It will. It'll have to. One way or the other.'

When he had waved Margaret off Edwin got his coat.

'I'll just have a walk round,' he said. 'Look for that lad.'

'Oh no.' Jean put her hand on his sleeve, and then, on reflection, took it away again. 'Is there any use? He must have gone deliberately.'

'I must try.'

'I'll go too,' said Philip.

'No.' Edwin looked at Jean's peaked face. 'Stay with your mother.'

'But . . .' The doorbell rang, silencing him.

'Well.' Jean flushed with relief. 'False alarm. Here he is. Thank goodness.'

But it was not Alfred who was waiting on the doorstep. It was David and Sheila; stricken.

'At this time of night . . .' said Jean. 'What are you two doing here?'

'Come in, come in.' Edwin closed the door behind them and switched the hall light on again. 'What is it? What's happened?'

'The kids,' said David. 'They were at Sheila's mother's. Staying the night.' He stopped talking and looked desperately at Sheila, who stared back as dumbly. 'Well,' Edwin prompted urgently. 'Well,' began David. He stopped again and gulped. 'Well, it's been hit. Bombed. And we can't find them.'

'Oh no.' Jean put her arm round Sheila, who had begun to sob quietly. Sheila turned her face into Jean's shoulder and her sobs grew louder. 'It's my fault. It's my fault,' she said.

'No, of course it isn't.' Jean patted Sheila's shoulder helplessly. 'Don't say that.'

'Take her in, take her in.' Edwin ushered them towards the lounge. 'We'll go ... Philip and me and David. We'll go and look. If we all go we should find something out.'

'We've looked.' David's voice was flat and weary. 'We've looked for hours. It's horrible out there.'

'Ssh.' Jean was covering Sheila's ears and rocking her back and forth. 'Quiet now. It could have happened anywhere. You weren't to know.'

'But I said ...' Sheila was gabbling between her sobs. 'I told Davy ... he's been going on and on about them being evacuated. He said something like this would happen. I couldn't stand him going on but I didn't want to send them away. So I said ... I told him. I said they'd gone to Wales. Only it was my mother had them. For company, and with me working. She didn't want them to be evacuated either. Only now ... it's my punishment.'

'Shut up, Sheila.' David patted her shoulder almost violently. 'It's not only your fault. I said a lot but I did nothing. Don't cry.'

'Tea,' said Jean. 'And bring all the sugar we've got, Philip. Then you can look. The men will look, Sheila. They'll find them. I'm sure they will.'

When the three men set out the night was over. It was already light but the air had none of the freshness of dawn. A fine dust hung everywhere, it sifted down out of the grey sky, smoky and harsh, making Edwin cough. It smelt of charred wood and bad eggs and gunpowder, a smell that Philip recalled with a shudder.

Edwin and Philip walked on either side of David as if to support him; as he walked he rolled a little and his shoulders banged theirs. He talked incessantly, compulsively, waving his hands and turning to stare first at his father and then at Philip as if he might find reassurance in their faces. But neither of them could manage as much as a smile.

As they got nearer to Mrs Rutherford's road the signs of the raid were unavoidable. They passed houses with their windows blown out, knots of dazed women with tired, drawn faces, and the smell of burning grew stronger.

'We were under the table,' David was saying. 'It was quite cosy, really. Sheila said did I want to go to the public shelter in Arkwright Street and I said no. I joked about it. I said I wanted my wife at home, not in one of them, and we were still laughing when there was this kind of scream and thump and the whole house shook. Sheila was laughing and then she started to cry, altogether just like that. And then she said the kids were at her mother's. She'd told me they were in Wales. I'd written and said I wanted them to go and she promised me she'd send them. I told her this would happen. I told her. Anyway we set off running. But Mrs Rutherford's was down. They wouldn't let us near. I told them it was my children but they wouldn't let us near. They were . . . digging.'

'All right, son, all right.' Edwin took David's arm as they turned the corner. 'Take it easy, David. I'm sure everybody is doing what they can.'

The end of the street had been cordoned off. A group of people stood by the rope barrier. A woman was weeping.

'What's happened?' said David. 'Perhaps they've found something.'

'Wait here,' said Edwin. 'Philip, stay with him. I'll find out what I can.'

Edwin pushed his way through the knot of people. Beyond them the view was curiously open; two rows of terraced houses that normally blocked it had been flattened so that Edwin could see beyond them to the heavy sky. The bricks from the houses lay all over the place in jagged mounds. The outside ones were the familiar grimy red but the inside ones, where the plaster had flaked off them, were a fresh pink, overlaid now by the grey dust that was drifting everywhere. The whole scene was unreal. The piled rubble looked too puny ever to have been habitable. Had it not been for the rescue team digging feverishly beneath a propped up door Edwin would have found it difficult to believe people had ever lived here at all.

He hailed an Air Raid Warden. The man was grimy and weary. Where his hat was pushed back up his forehead clean skin showed like a wound.

'Yes?' he said.

'Number eight,' Edwin said. 'Mrs Rutherford's. Do you know anything about who was in there?'

'Relative, are you?'

'My grandchildren . . . it's my son, over there, his mother-in-law.'

'Him,' said the Warden. 'He was round at the post in the night, wasn't he?'

'That's right.'

'Has he looked in the shelters. I told him to look in the shelters.'

'He's looked everywhere,' said Edwin. 'He's been looking all night.'

The man looked at Edwin with sympathy and lowered his voice.

'To tell you the truth we don't know who's here and who's not. They got some people out of number five. And an old man out of number two but . . .' The man shrugged and jerked his thumb towards the ground.

Edwin looked from that despairing gesture along the shattered street again. A gust of wind that swirled the dust clouds higher and carried the acrid smell of destruction so far into his throat that he gasped and choked, blew a torn piece of lace curtain round his ankles so that when he took a step away he almost fell. Behind him a woman started to cry.

'Thanks, anyway,' said Edwin to the man, and turned away to go back to David. He was bracing himself to be cheerful and optimistic, but that was not how he felt. He felt tired and old and frightened. He had seen death and destruction before, but that had been in the trenches. There only men had died. Here it was women and children too.

Edwin and his sons made another long, slow tour of the shelters and the warden's posts but to no avail. Nobody seemed to remember seeing David's children. Edwin began to worry about Jean.

'We'd better go home,' he said. 'We can come back later.'

'No.' David was exhausted but determined. 'I won't come. If I'm here they might see me . . . if they're lost or something. I must stay here.'

In the end Edwin and Philip had to leave him to stand and wait at the makeshift barrier.

'Will you be all right?' asked Edwin. 'Your mother . . .'

'Go on,' said David. 'I'll be all right. Go and tell Sheila ... I'll wait for them.'

But Sheila was asleep when they got back. Only Jean, spruce in spite of her sleepless night, was in the kitchen. She cooked them some breakfast while they told her what they knew.

'Oh well. We'll just have to hope,' she said.

'What about Margaret?' Philip asked.

'No news yet. There wouldn't be.'

'Wouldn't there? I don't know.'

'Well, there wouldn't be.'

'And that lad?' asked Edwin.

'Alfred? Huh.' Jean wiped her wet hands and sat down at the table opposite him. 'No need to worry about him.'

'He's been found?'

'Not yet, but he will be. Jack Sanderson's on the job. And his mother's coming. They've traced her.'

'But will he be all right?'

'I think that one can look after himself,' Jean said. 'He's not an evacuee after all. It turns out he simply hopped it off his own bat.'

'Ran away?' asked Philip. 'Why should he do that?'

'To look for his father.' Jean looked sad. 'Or rather his father's grave, the sea. His father's dead, he was in a convoy, and his mother ... Jack said she didn't seem to care. She seems to be rather a rough type of woman.'

'I see.' Edwin caught Philip's grimace at this sign of Jean's tendency to snobbishness. There was, as Edwin had once told her, all bark and no bite about it. She categorised people in their absence but when she was face to face with them she forgot all her disapproval. He had no doubt that when Alfred's mother turned up Jean would be as welcoming to her as she was to her own family.

And so it was. When she came, Alfred's mother, with her lurid hair and her gaudy coat, was put in the best chair and given tea out of the best cups. The police rang just before she arrived to say that Alfred had been found in Wallasey, and Philip was despatched to fetch him. Mrs Powner waited for him unconcernedly. Edwin was glad that she had come. So long as she was there, prattling about her dead husband and the man she proposed, with what Jean considered indecent haste, to marry, she was some sort of company for Jean. Her conversation, trivial though it was, kept Jean's mind from brooding over Peter and Janet. Because Mrs Powner was there Edwin felt himself free to go back and help David with his vigil.

Alfred was rather subdued when Philip found him.

'It's big,' he said, indicating the river as they stood on the deck of the ferry on the way home.

'This is only the estuary,' said Philip. 'You should see the sea. That's out there beyond the river mouth.'

'That's the sea?' Alfred looked intently along the line of Philip's pointing finger.'

'Yes.'

'Is it very big?'

'Vast. Unimaginably big.'

'Is this the nearest we get to it?'

'On this boat, yes.'

'Are you sure?' Alfred was very concerned to establish that.

'Yes,' said Philip, 'I'm sure.'

'Well, then.' Alfred drew from his pocket a crumpled packet of cigarettes. He looked at Philip sidelong, with his odd mixture of caution and bravado.

'Where did you get those?' Philip asked suspiciously.

Alfred looked down at his shuffling feet. 'I found them.'

Philip remembered, from what seemed now a long time ago in the middle of that noisy night, a frantic hunt for Edwin's cigarettes.

'Where did you find them?'

Alfred shuffled his feet harder and said nothing.

'Tell me where.' Philip's indignation welled up. How dared this child, to whom in the middle of problems of their own, his parents had extended their hospitality, so abuse it.

He was mustering words for his attack when Alfred, with a gesture, disarmed him. The boy stood on tiptoe and stretched out his thin arm as far as he could across the painted rail of the ferry boat, suspending the crushed packet over the churned water.

'My dad's in there,' he said, staring down at the ochre waves.

'In there?'

'In the sea. Drowned.'

'Oh.'

'And these are for him.'

A cold wind blew up from the river mouth. Alfred, in his thin jacket, shivered. 'This is his cemetery, isn't it? The cigarettes are like a wreath. There's only me to bother. My mam didn't.'

'I see.' Philip thought of corpses rolling on the sea-bed as the water heaved. He had never liked the sea. He put his arm across Alfred's shoulder and said: 'Throw them in.'

'Will it be all right?' the boy asked anxiously. 'Only he'd like cigarettes better than flowers.'

'It'll be all right.'

'Shall I say a prayer?'

'If you like.'

'I only know one.' Alfred stood on tiptoe to look deeper into the water. His thin arm shook with the effort of his reach and his shoulders felt frail under Philip's arm.

'For what we are about to receive,' he said, gabbling so that Philip could hardly hear, 'may the Lord make us truly thankful.'

It was ten o'clock when Edwin got back to David but the scene was much the same. David turned as he felt his father's hand on his shoulder and shook his head.

'No news?' asked Edwin.

'Oh well, you know what they say, no news is good news.'

'Is it?'

'Come home for something to eat.'

'I'd rather not. Somebody might know. I saw Billy Chetwynd from next door half an hour back. He said he saw her last night, Mrs Rutherford, before it started, but not since. He said they might have been in the Wagstaffe's shelter.'

'Did you go?'

'I ran. But they hadn't seen them.'

A whistle blew and the noise of the crane's engine stopped. A policeman came towards the knot of people at the cordon and held his hand up.

'Could we have silence everybody, please,' he said. 'They're listening to see if they can hear anything. Knocking or shouting.'

It was so quiet that Edwin could hear the sound of David's

breathing, and the pip of a tug's hooter from far away on the river. A little stream of plaster that fell suddenly from a crack in a leaning wall splattered to the ground with disconcerting loudness. The silence was so unnerving that Edwin wanted to shout out loud. Then the whistle blew again, and among the knot of waiting people there seemed to be a corporate drawing of breath as they all prepared themselves to start talking again. But before the hubbub could build up Edwin heard from somewhere behind him the high, clear shouting of a child's voice.

David swung round as suddenly and disjointedly as a marionette on a string. Then he lunged forward down the road before Edwin could even turn his head, and let out a great shout.

Hope gave springs to Edwin's legs. He turned and started to run after David. A small figure ran round the corner towards David. It was a boy, dishevelled and dirty and screaming with delight. It was Peter.

By the time Edwin reached him both the children were clinging to David as though he were their liferaft. Sheila's mother panted round the corner and began her explanations before she got her breath back. Nothing that any of them were saying that could be heard made any sense.

Edwin looked behind him at the group of people at the barrier, those who were still waiting in vain. All of them were staring at the rejoicing David. Edwin cleared his throat and drew on his authority.

'Let's get back,' he said. 'We should tell Sheila and Jean. And have something to eat. We can talk there.'

Jean cried when she saw them. She, who could be so brave and sensible in a crisis, usually cried when it was over. Sheila, roused from a drugged sleep, was calm and beatific. She hugged her children close as Edwin and David questioned her mother about where they had all been.

'In Plunkett's shelter. With Frank and Herbert away they've got plenty of room.'

'Yes, but why didn't you come out? We expected you all the time after the All Clear. We waited. We looked. It was awful.'

'We fell asleep, that's all. And Mrs Plunkett left us. She didn't think about anybody wondering. And I did tell Mrs Janes across the street where we was. I didn't know she'd be . . .'

'Yes, yes, it's all right.' In his relief David didn't want to dwell on someone else's sorrow. 'It couldn't be helped. It's all right now you're back. Now you're safe.'

'Davy was right,' said Sheila. 'The children should go somewhere safe, away from here.'

'Thank goodness,' said David. 'Then my mind will be at rest.'

'Will mine?' asked Sheila.

'You can't hope for that, Sheila,' Jean said. 'You can't hope not to worry. Not at a time like this. Just hope not to grieve. That's the best we can expect.'

CHAPTER EIGHT

Late that afternoon Margaret gave birth to a baby boy. Jean had the news to herself for some time. She had telephoned the hospital with increasing frequency all day usually to be told that there was, as yet, no news. So when at last the answering voice said 'Mrs Porter ... a baby boy ... both well ...' Jean could hardly believe it. The news seemed to her too good to be true.

All that night and all the morning she had lived in the shadow of disaster. Each reprieve from what she had dreaded had not lessened her fear, it had simply concentrated it on what was left to dread. So that once all the family had survived the night and Sheila's children had been found Jean had been certain, though she would not have admitted it to anyone, that something dreadful must happen to Margaret.

But it had not. Margaret had a son and both she and her baby were well. Suddenly all Jean's fears fell from her. She felt light headed and joyful, dizzy with relief. She wanted to talk and talk, to tell everybody the good news. She telephoned Edwin's office eagerly. But he was not there.

'I'll phone later,' she said. 'No, I won't leave a message.' She wanted to tell Edwin about his grandson herself.

She thought of other people she could tell. The Porters, but they weren't on the phone. Freda, but she was at work. Sheila and David, but they had gone round to their house to collect some things. Philip, but he was out. Robert, but he was at school.

Suddenly Jean felt very very tired. The effort of getting in touch with any of those people seemed too great. She would sit down, just for a minute, and then she would phone Edwin again.

Edwin found her asleep in the chair when he got home. He was shaking her shoulder to rouse her when Freda and Philip came in.

'Very nice, too,' said Freda, surveying her bemused mother. 'I wish I could do that. I've been too keyed up wondering about our Margaret all day to sit still, even.'

'She's tired out,' said Edwin. 'I was just going to ring the hospital and I thought she might like to be with me to hear the news if there is any.'

'Hospital?' said Jean sleepily. 'News? Oh yes, good, isn't it?'

'I'm going to phone,' said Edwin. 'It's taking a long time.'

'A little boy,' said Jean. 'Just what she wanted. And we can visit at seven.'

'Is that it?' Edwin asked, 'You mean, you know.'

'Oh, Mum.' Freda started to laugh. 'You knew all the time what we were longing to hear, and all you did was sleep.'

'Sleep?' said Jean. 'Oh, I am sorry.'

Suddenly they were all laughing and talking at once.

'A boy. Lovely. And Margaret well.'

'Sleeping like a . . . like a baby.'

'You know, Mum, they'll never let you forget this,' said Philip.

Even Margaret teased her about it when, in the awkward pause that came after the first rush of congratulations as they sat at her bedside that evening, Edwin told her about it.

'Oh, Mum,' she said. 'Fancy not staying awake to tell them. After I'd worked so hard all day.'

'I didn't mean to fall asleep,' said Jean. 'Really I was thinking who to tell first. But I just couldn't keep my eyes open. It was the relief, I suppose, after . . .'

Edwin kicked Jean's ankle. 'After the raid,' he said. They had decided not to tell Margaret about Janet and Peter. It would only worry her, and she was going to have enough to worry about without that.

Within a week the children were evacuated. Sheila prepared to send them away with the same resolution that she had used to keep them with her, taking time off work to scour the shops to find new clothes for them.

'I'll not have anybody thinking they're slum children,' she said to Jean fiercely, 'even if they've not had much before this. Some of the kids have gone because their mothers didn't care. I'll not have anybody think that of mine.' She was on the verge of tears and Jean tried to soothe her.

'Of course nobody'll think that, Sheila. And they're not going very far. You can write to them, and visit.'

'I've heard what some people say about evacuee kids,' said Sheila. 'I want mine to go with everything nice.'

'They'll be safer in the country this winter,' said Jean. 'I don't know . . . I don't think we've had the worst yet, Sheila. I'm sure you're doing the right thing. And at least you won't be on your own now your mother's coming to stay with you.'

'No, I suppose not. But my mother's not the same as my kids, is she? It's not how I thought I was going to end up when I got married. I think to myself that if only I could just have us all together again, me and David and the children, I'd never grumble again.'

'Well,' said Jean, with an optimism she did not feel, 'you'll be able to remember that when you are all together again. Then perhaps all this will have done a bit of good after all.'

But it was noticeable that once the children had gone David's visits home were less frequent. This was partly due to pressure of work.

As the autumn drew on and the nights grew longer he was flying on more and more bombing missions. The Germans were, too. People grew used to the sound of aircraft. They listened to their droning engines and told each other whether the noise was made by one of 'ours' going or one of 'theirs' coming.

Jean pondered on the irony of it. While her son was risking his life to bomb Germany boys like him but with a different language were coming to bomb children like his! It seemed to her foolish, but she did not say so. In the autumn of nineteen forty thoughts like that would not have been popular.

On the rare occasions when David did get home he was not

very good company. He talked all the time in a R.A.F. jargon that the rest of the family found strange. Jean tried to ease the situation by turning the talk to personalities, but that was not always a good idea.

'How's ... what's his name?' she asked. 'Jack something or other ... Reynolds. Your pilot, I think you said.'

'He's dead,' said David.

'Oh. Oh, David, I am sorry.'

'It happens.'

'Yes, but ... you never mentioned.'

'I wasn't there. It was when I had my bad finger. We've had quite a change round in the crew since I saw you last. He's not the only one ... we don't go out on joy rides, you know.'

'I never thought you did, David.'

'No. I'm sorry, Mum. I didn't mean to say that. Only it seems so different here from down at the base.'

'It's not exactly safe here,' said Margaret.

'No. Only I can't help feeling a bit bitter because two of my mates copped it from our own side. One's dead. The other ... his hands were burned off. All because of the trigger-happy shore batteries when we'd dropped our load and thought we were safely home.'

Jean went very white and put her hand up to her head. Margaret got up from her chair and went over to her mother.

'I'll fetch the baby down, shall I?' she said. 'It's nearly his feed time and I'm sure Sheila and David would like to see him before they go. Wouldn't you, Sheila?'

Sheila, who was sitting huddled close to David, nodded.

'Yes, please, Margaret. Then we must go. Try not to think about ... all that ... when you're at home, Davy.' Sheila looked thinner than ever, and clung to David with desperate intensity, holding his arm even as he kissed his mother good night.

Yet David hardly seemed to notice her. It seemed to Margaret that he put up with Sheila's clinging hands more because he didn't notice than because he welcomed them. Margaret didn't like to see Sheila like that. For one thing it exacerbated her own loneliness, pointing to the fact that she herself had no one to cling to. But as well as that she hated to see Sheila so dependent for Sheila's own sake. David had never been a very dependable person.

What Philip had to say didn't reassure her. Philip was on a gunnery course and had been posted quite near to David. The two of them met from time to time whenever their free evenings coincided, though the meetings were more, Margaret thought, on account of Jean's urging than from any volition of either Philip or David.

Philip was Jean's link with David. As David grew away from the family on which he had used to depend so much so Philip drew closer to the rest of them. Philip had talked more to his mother now than ever he had done when he was away at Oxford or setting off to fight in Spain. The simple black and white of the situation suited Philip. It was easy at this time in the war for him to decide who was right and who was wrong. He liked to be able for once to hold the same views as everybody around him. It was a relief to him to do rather than to think. On his visits home he enjoyed being one of the family again instead of the odd one out as he had sometimes been before.

Margaret, privately, asked him more searching questions about David than Jean did. Jean was content to know that David was well, that he seemed happy, that he had friends, that his missions weren't too dangerous. Margaret was blunter.

'Philip,' she asked, when they were on their own in the house one afternoon, 'is David carrying on with someone?'

She knew from the way Philip jumped that she was on to the right track. But he said blandly: 'I don't know what you mean.'

'I mean,' said Margaret, 'another woman.'

'What makes you ask that?'

'He's different, you must have noticed it. He's different with Sheila. Before they were always either cat and dog or lovey dovey. Now there's none of that. He's kind of not bothered about her any more.'

'He's seen men die. It makes you hard.'

'Are you sure that's all? I know you don't want to tell tales. I know it's a man's world down there. But I think someone should keep an eye on David.'

'There's school marm Margaret talking.'

'I'm asking a straight question. If you don't give me a straight answer I'm bound to think the worst, aren't I?'

'Well, then, I'll tell you what I know, if you insist. Not that there's anything to tell, really. So far as I know there's only one girl down there that David really knows. Actually she's the widow of an old oppo of his, his pilot. Her name is Susan Reynolds and she works for the W.V.S. running a study centre. I must say I was a bit surprised when it came out that David had taken up studying history.'

'Has he? Well, well. He never told us that. So there must be something in it.'

'I never said so. I know nothing about it. Perhaps he is keen on her, but she's not his type. She's better educated, altogether different. Don't mention her to anyone. There may be nothing to mention. They're just friends. She's friends with a lot of the boys down there. I'm sure it'll all come to nothing.'

'Let's hope so,' said Margaret. 'Let's hope so, for Sheila's sake.'

Margaret's son, John George, was the apple of everybody's eye. He grew fat and cheerful, in spite of the fact that his nights were disturbed by air raids and his days, until Margaret put her foot down, by the too frequent attentions of Jean, Edwin and Freda.

'That child will get spoilt,' Margaret declared. 'He's not to be picked up the minute he cries, he must learn to wait until feed time. Really, Mum, you should know better.'

'It's so nice to have a baby in the house again,' Jean said. 'And he's such a good baby. Just like Robert was.'

'He won't be good if he's spoilt, though, will he?'

'No, I suppose you're right.'

'And Freda's not to have him out the minute she comes in from work either. She can do what she likes when she has one of her own, but I won't have her spoiling John George.'

'Tell her that,' said Edwin, laughing. 'It might encourage her to get married.'

'Oh, Dad, you're hopeless. Why should she get married. She's happy as she is.'

'Is she?' said Edwin. 'I don't know. I suppose all parents like to see their daughters married. Stupid of me, really.'

'Well, I can't see that Freda's in the mood to take the plunge just yet, can you?'

'No, I suppose not. Though I often think that Peter Collins would be willing enough if she gave him a chance.'

'I daresay you're right. But I can't say I blame Freda for not being too keen. When all's said and done it's not exactly exciting, is it, marrying the boy next door?'

'Next door but four,' said Jean.

'Oh, Mum. As if that's the point.'

The point was that Freda had outgrown Peter Collins. She had been friendly with him for most of her life. The two of them had played with their teddy bears together at the age of three, gone to school together at the age of five, gone for bike rides together at the age of ten and kissed each other experimentally at the age of thirteen.

But after that Freda had changed and Peter had not. When Freda had found that out in the world she could hold her own in an interesting and varied job she had developed poise and self-confidence and a rather febrile need for excitement that Peter would never be able to meet. Peter's quiet diffident and over-anxiety to please irritated Freda now. Margaret could see, even if Jean could not, that Jean's long cherished plan for Freda settling down with Peter would never come to fruition.

Peter couldn't see it either. With dogged persistence, and egged on by Jean, he continued to ask Freda to go out with him. He worked in the same small office that he had gone to straight from school and his widowed mother sheltered him, the more so since her elder son had joined the Navy. He had very little experience of the world so to him the more distant Freda grew the more desirable she seemed, the more dismissive she was with him the more determined he became.

The whole situation came to a head one evening in November. At the beginning of the month Freda changed her job. She had done so, in spite of her mother's protests, partly out of a feeling of restlessness and partly out of a genuine desire to do something more useful than be nice to wealthy businessmen eating out to spare their rations. 'Fiddling,' as Freda put it, 'while Liverpool burns.' She became a clerk in the wages department of a factory that made munitions; the factory worked shifts round the clock and Freda, on the second shift, was usually not home until the late evening.

On one of these evenings Margaret sent Peter out to meet Freda's bus. He had been at the Ashtons since teatime, listening to the radio, talking to Jean, patiently waiting for Freda. He would be better off, Margaret thought, steering Freda through the blackout than just sitting there. She couldn't have known how wrong she was because she didn't know about Owen.

Freda had only known Owen for a week, but in a time of hail and farewell, of short leaves and long absences that was enough. Owen was Australian and an airman; he had all the outgoing confidence and charm that Peter lacked. He had quite literally, bumped into Freda in the panicky dark when an air raid siren had sounded one night when she was on her way home from work. He had taken charge at once, steered her to a shelter and eventually seen her home. The attraction was mutual. After that Owen had met Freda out of work and walked her home every night for a week.

Freda had deliberately not mentioned him to the family. The fact that Owen was private to her was part of his appeal. Since Robert had been away at school Freda had been the youngest one at home and it wasn't a position she altogether enjoyed. It seemed to her that David and Margaret and Philip were allowed a freedom of action that she was not. So by seeing Owen clandestinely she was making a gesture towards independence.

Besides, she wanted to protect the burgeoning relationship between them from her mother's too keen interest. She got on well with Owen, she was flattered by the attention he gave her, and she was conscious of how short a time they had together. More than that she did not know. But her mother would be bound to ask for more. So Freda kept her meetings with Owen secret.

It was Peter who spoiled it all. After he had been sent out by Margaret he walked down towards the bus stop looking for Freda. He saw her at the worst possible moment.

Freda opened her eyes after Owen's kiss and saw Peter's face looming from the darkness over Owen's shoulder. She could see at once from his expression how surprised and shocked he was and thought there would be trouble. Even so she wasn't prepared for what followed.

With a cry of rage and misery Peter launched himself at Owen. Owen, unprepared, reeled under the attack. Freda tried to get between them but Peter was flailing his arms like a madman and yelling abuse indiscriminately at Owen and at Freda. Freda only managed to grasp Owen's hand and at that moment Peter's fist landed on Owen's face with a crack like a gunshot.

The sight of blood quietened Peter down. Freda, sobbing, helped Owen to his feet. 'Look what you've done,' she said to Peter. 'He's hurt. Have you gone mad? Help me. I'm going to take him home.'

So the first the family knew of Owen was when he appeared on their doorstep, muddy and shaken and bleeding from the nose and from a cut on his lip. To Jean's credit she found him a chair and a clean towel before she asked questions.

'Now then,' she said, when Freda was bathing Owen's face. 'What has been going on?'

Freda was shaking with shock and fury. 'There's been a fight. In the street. It was horrible.'

'But what was it to do with you? Do you know this ... young man?'

'Yes, I do.'

'But how? Who is he?'

Owen, recovering a little, spoke up for himself. 'I'm sorry about this,' he said. 'Don't get me wrong. I didn't start it.'

'Who did then? And what are you to do with Freda?'

Freda, calmer now that she had seen that the damage to Owen was less than it had seemed, looked embarrassed.

'It's a long story, Mum,' she said.

Jean didn't take the explanation very well. Her sympathy, as she made plain to Freda, lay mainly with Peter.

'But, Mum,' Freda protested. 'He hit first. He was like an animal. He had no right. He has no right to me.'

'He's always been fond of you. You should have told him. About ... about Owen here. You should have told us all.'

Margaret came to Freda's rescue.

'To be fair, Mother,' she said, 'I think Freda did try to let Peter know she wasn't interested. But he wouldn't take the hint. Peter's what you'd call the dogged type. It's not easy to get him to change his mind.'

Just how dogged Peter was Jean found out the next day. She accepted, in the end, Owen's good faith towards Freda. Indeed, she ended the evening feeling quite cordial towards him. Even so, she insisted that Freda must speak to Peter and offer him an explanation.

For the sake of peace Freda agreed, but she refused to go to

Peter's house.

'I can't, Mum,' she said. 'I won't see him in front of his mother. She's never liked me, you know that, and if she's just heard his side of the story and not mine she'll be unbearable.'

'All right.' Jean was willing to go some way towards Freda now that Freda was willing to be reconciled with Peter. 'I'll go down and ask him to come up here. Just so long as you promise to be nice to him.'

'I'll be as nice as I can,' Freda said. 'But just on a friendly basis. I'm not . . . keen on Peter. Owen . . . I like him better.'

Peter seemed positively eager to go and see Freda when Jean arrived at his house to say that Freda was at home.

'There are things,' he said, 'I want to say to her.' And for once his mother didn't attempt to stop him going out. She was only too anxious to get Jean on her own.

Jean had always found Mrs Collins an irritating woman. She put up a façade of helpless femininity as a device for getting her own way, making a small mishap into a disaster, a larger one into a tragedy. But this morning her familiar agitation seemed greater than usual. Underneath the old tricks of fluttering fingers and moist eyes Jean sensed this time real desperation. Because instead of bursting out as she usually did with a flood of words about her troubles Mrs Collins simply stared at Jean.

Jean felt uncomfortable. She shifted in her chair and looked round the room. Then she cleared her throat and said: 'Not too cold, for November, is it?'

Mrs Collins' hand flung wide in a gesture of despair and she said: 'It's all your Freda's fault.'

Like a vixen Jean defended her own.

'Oh, I don't think so. At least she didn't hit anyone.'

'Oh that,' Mrs Collins dismissed the fight. 'That's not the worst, is it? What about my Peter going to join the Navy?'

'Peter? But that's impossible,' Jean said. 'He's not . . . the type. And besides I thought that draughtsmen were reserved.'

'So they are. He has no need to go. But he says he will and it's all because of Freda, because of the way she's treated him. As if I haven't given enough. My Danny's already at sea. I can't give them Peter too. How shall I manage, a woman alone? Did she think of that, Freda? Did she?'

'Mrs Collins,' said Jean, 'I think we should remember that

Peter's grown up. He's a man now, he knows his own mind.'

'He's not more than a boy. Not really. He's always been my little boy. And how can he know his own mind when she's driven him out of it? She's driven him mad.'

'You must be mad,' Freda was saying to Peter. She had dreaded this meeting, but she had agreed to it to please her mother and because it did seem only fair to Peter that she should see him. In the cold light of the morning after she was forced to admit that the meetings with Owen that to her were so romantic and exciting could seem to other people deceitful and underhand. So she had agreed to talk to Peter and even to offer him an apology. She had expected similar concessions from him. Instead what she got was abuse.

'You were like a tart,' Peter had said. 'Standing in a doorway letting him do what he liked. You're all alike, aren't you, just going for the uniform, not caring about decency or about decent fellows. I should have seen through you long ago.'

And Freda, stunned, could only say: 'You must be mad,' before he was off again.

'Who is he, anyway? Nobody. An Australian. Coming here to steal our girls just because he's dressed in Air Force blue.' In his agitation he was walking up and down. His face was red and his mouth stretched into an ugly square. Freda tried to speak, to defend herself, but Peter did not stop to listen. He just went on talking, his voice overriding hers, his words almost incoherent because of the vehemence with which he was speaking.

'Well, if that's how you see things,' he said. 'If you can't see the wood from the trees, if what you want is a fancy uniform I'll get one too. I'm going to join the Navy. That'll show you, that'll make me as good as the rest of them.'

'Peter, no.' Freda was genuinely appalled. 'Think before you do a thing like that,' she pleaded. 'You've got it all wrong. It wasn't ... like you say with me and Owen. It's not just the uniform, it's him I like. Don't do anything hasty, Peter.'

But Peter was not to be dissuaded by anyone. Neither his mother's tears nor Freda's pleading would change his mind. Jean tried to talk to him about it but he did not listen. He had made up his mind that to join the Navy would be the answer to all his problems, that by donning a uniform he would at once acquire the self-confidence and respect that he could not otherwise get.

Jean was very concerned. She had defended Freda's part in the matter to Mrs Collins but to Edwin she confided her real feelings.

'Freda could have behaved better. If only she'd been straight with us all perhaps this would never have happened. I suppose it's partly my fault. I did push them at each other a bit I suppose. If I hadn't Peter mightn't feel so strongly. You'll see him this evening at the A.R.P. post, won't you? Try and get him to think again. I can't help feeling a bit responsible.'

Peter, unlike Edwin, was a properly trained part-time warden and was on duty at the post most evenings. It was an excuse to get away from his mother. Ted Fiddler, the full-time warden, was always trying to persuade Edwin to take the training course and come on to the regular duty rota but Edwin declined. Now that he was in name as well as in fact manager at the works he felt it his duty to take turns firewatching there a couple of nights a week and he wanted to be free to spend some time in the evenings with Jean. He thought that if he was committed to regular duty he might have to leave her when she needed him most; as it was he did the best he could to juggle his various commitments so as to do the best for everyone.

Except of course for himself. Edwin was no longer young. The strain of sleepless nights on top of the constant anxiety he felt on behalf of Margaret and his sons was beginning to tell. He was furious with Freda for introducing the further complication of Peter. It's about time, he thought to himself, that that young woman grew up. If it hadn't been for Jean's worried face he would have preferred to wash his hands of the whole matter.

Peter was already at the post when Edwin arrived, sticking coloured pins into the Area map to bring it up to date. The post was in what used to be a secondhand clothes shop, converted now by its blacked-out windows and sandbagged door into a safe haven. It smelt perpetually of tea and wet clothing and long use had given it, in spite of the dim light and makeshift furniture, an air of cosiness. But Peter, that evening, didn't seem at ease there. His ill-fitting boiler suit and the armband that had slipped awkwardly down on to his elbow gave him the air of a waif. Edwin felt sorry for the boy. He determined to talk some sense into him, to try and dissuade him from joining up.

Conditions at the post were not really conducive to a quiet talk. Edwin took what opportunities he could, drawing Peter away to a quiet corner when there was not much going on and taking advantage of Ted Fiddler's absences to speak with more force. But it was no use. Peter seemed quite immovable. He had made his mind up, and closed it.

Just before ten o'clock the phone rang with a red warning and within minutes the air-raid siren started its moan. Ted Fiddler came back from his patrol outside and organised his resources.

'Peter,' he said. 'You'll have to go out. There's a bedroom window showing a light in Dove Street. I couldn't get an answer when I rang the bell so I think it'll come to climbing in. It'll have to be you that does it. My climbing days are over, and I think I can say the same for Mr Ashton. But make it quick.'

Peter put on his steel helmet. Under the shadow of its rim his unhappy face looked more haunted still. Edwin put a hand on his shoulder.

'Cheer up, lad,' he said. 'Nothing lasts. You'll have forgotten all about this business and about Freda too, in a month or so. Believe me.'

Those were the last words anybody said to Peter Collins.

The bomb that killed him fell less than a minute after he had left the shelter of the post. Ted and Edwin heard it fall, they felt the force of its explosion and cowered instinctively as the building shook. Then the noise began to fade and they knew they had not been hit; by common consent they raised their heads as soon as they dared and made their way outside. They were picking their way over the debris in the doorway almost before the dust had begun to rise. But that was too late for Peter. They stumbled upon his body ten yards along the road. It took the strength of three men to lift the beam that had crushed the life out of him.

CHAPTER NINE

Edwin broke the news about Peter as gently as he could to Freda. He knew how much of a shock it would be to her. She listened in silence and afterwards went away to her room. She never mentioned Peter's name again. She was trying to forget about the whole business.

But it changed her. After Peter's death Freda would not walk past his house; instead she went round three sides of the block to the bus stop every morning. She laughed less. From a careless, carefree girl she had changed into a hard, flippant woman.

Edwin did not like the change. He did not like any of the changes that war had brought to his family. He did not like the way that Jean had become sharp with the effort to make ends meet or the way that Margaret had grown dour through living without her husband. He did not like the way in which some men, like Sefton, could use their money to cushion themselves against the war. There were bright spots, it was true. He enjoyed the feeling of pulling together with the men at work, and he liked the responsibility of being a warden albeit an occasional one. But all these things were outweighed by his constant fear for his children. He feared for them all, and increasingly for Robert now that his years at Nautical School were coming to an end.

Robert was Jean's baby, the youngest of the family. But he was sixteen and a half now, and leaving childhood behind. He had spent the last few years learning to be a sailor. Now the learning was over and the real thing was about to begin. At the end of term he arrived home for the last time. He brought the accumulated clutter of those years back with him. Margaret went through the mound sorting out what might be useful for salvage while Jean exclaimed in pleased horror at the piles of washing and mending he produced for her.

Robert had been home on holiday fairly frequently but somehow it was only now that he had finished at school that Jean and Edwin were able to see how different the Robert who had come back to them was from the timid child who had gone away. Robert now, though he still looked like a boy, was a man. He still had the open face and stick wrists of a child but he was as tall as his father and as strong. He had a man's certainty. He knew what he wanted to do.

He brought home with him a youthful gaiety and zest that were like a tonic to his war-weary family. He brought a new light into Jean's eyes and smiles to even Margaret's lips as he teased and clowned and played with the baby. He also brought with him his enlistment papers for Edwin to sign.

He approached Edwin with them diffidently one evening when Jean was out at a First Aid Class.

'Dad,' he began seriously, 'I've been thinking about the future.'

'Have you, Robert?' Edwin said. 'Not many people can manage to think further ahead than tomorrow, these days.'

'Oh, I don't mean the distant future,' Robert said. 'Not ... after the war and all that. Just about what I'm going to do now. After Christmas.'

'I see,' said Edwin, and his heart sank. 'What do you have in mind?'

'I want to go to sea,' Robert said.

'I was afraid you would.'

'I've got the papers here,' he said. 'I'll show you where you have to sign.'

'Whoa a minute, young Robert.' Edwin wondered what to do. 'I like a little time to think before I put my name to anything.'

Robert smiled wheedlingly. 'But you will, Dad, won't you?' he said. 'They won't take me without your consent, at my age.'

'Oh, Robert.' Edwin thought of Jean. She had been brave and sensible when David and Philip had gone to war but Robert was her baby. 'I don't know what your mother will say.'

'I waited until she'd gone out to ask you.'

'At least you've learned tact, then, at school.'

'I've learned a lot. I'm ready to go to sea. Just sign the papers, Dad.'

'Your mother won't like it.'

'It's what I've been trained for, isn't it? Why did she let me go to that school in the first place if she didn't want me to go to sea?'

'There wasn't a war on then,' Edwin said.

Robert, joking, took up a heroic pose. 'All the more reason now. The country needs me.'

'Robert, this is a serious matter. You might be . . . you know what your mother is afraid of as well as I do.'

'Yes, I do.' Suddenly Robert was mature beyond his years. 'Don't think I haven't thought of it. But I couldn't be happy with myself if I didn't do something, Dad. I am old enough to do my bit and I want to. It's my life and I know what I want to do with it.'

'All right, then.' Reluctantly Edwin picked up a pen and signed his name. 'But, Robert, don't tell your mother the matter's settled until I've had a word with her. I'll need to choose my moment, so just keep quiet. All right?'

'All right,' said Robert. He had got his way.

Robert was cock-a-hoop at the thought of going to sea. At school he had been imbued with the idea of patriotism and he was at an age when feelings run high. His love for his country was not, as was Edwin's and Philips, alloyed by any knowledge of her imperfections. He longed to play his part. The thought of danger, far from putting him off, excited him. To be a sailor would be a sure way of asserting the manhood that he was not always as sure of as he seemed. He acknowledged his mother's fears for him without understanding them. With the vitality of youth he thought it impossible that anything could happen to him.

He had meant to keep his promise to Edwin not to mention the matter to Jean but his enthusiasm got the better of him. One day without thinking he said: 'Perhaps I'll go to America. What shall I bring you back, Mum?'

'To America?' Jean said. 'Why?'

'If that's where my ship . . .'

'Ship? What ship?'

'Oh, I'm sorry, Mum.'

'What ship, Robert? You can't go in the Navy without your father's consent. I thought you might wait . . . see if it's what you want. They're short of workers at Freda's factory.'

'But I want to go to sea, Mum. It's what I've been trained for. All the other boys will go.'

'I don't want . . . you must speak to your father . . .' Jean saw Robert's face. 'Robert, you haven't asked him already?

What did he say?'

'He said ... I'm nearly seventeen, Mum.'

'Only sixteen, you mean.'

'I'd be ashamed if I didn't go.'

'You can't go.' Jean was determined. 'I shall speak to your father. Robert, it isn't safe.'

Edwin tried to explain to Jean why he could not refuse to sign Robert's papers.

'It's not fair to the boy. He has his pride. He has the right to do what he thinks he should.'

'But at his age. He's only sixteen. How can he know what he wants?'

'I'd been three years at work when I was his age. I knew what I wanted. It's his future, he has a right to fight for it if he wants to. It would be wrong of me to stop him.'

'Can't you persuade him? You must persuade him.'

'He won't be persuaded.'

'Well, then, you must insist.'

'I can't insist, Jean. There comes a time when you have to let him grow up. He's lived away from home. He's older in a way than the others were at the same age and David wasn't much more than seventeen when he got married ... you'll only keep your son by letting him go.'

'It's easy for you, isn't it?' Jean was bitter. 'You don't care as much as I do. If you did you wouldn't have signed him away so easily. If you cared for me you'd have made him stay at home.'

Edwin was weary and distressed. 'You're not the only one who doesn't like it,' he said. 'I have feelings too. I've had a lot of feelings over the years that I've kept to myself for your sake. Not only feelings about the children ... feelings about myself, about what I would have liked to do if I hadn't been prevented. And the person who prevented me was you. Perhaps you didn't mean to, but you have stood in my way, Jean, and I haven't always liked it. So I can see how Robert feels. I can stick up for him. I can stop the same thing happening to him. He can go if he wants to, Jean. I won't let you stop him.'

So Edwin began the crack that was to grow into a rift between himself and Jean.

For three peaceful weeks at the beginning of December no bombs had been dropped on Liverpool. Thankfully everybody took the chance to catch up on their lost sleep.

'You're all looking so much better,' said Jean after a week of undisturbed nights. 'A bit longer like this and we'll be ready to face anything, I'm sure.'

But she was wrong. When the raids did start again four days before Christmas it was as if there had never been a respite. Second time around the cycle of wailing sirens, crashing bombs and fear seemed harder to bear.

'It's like a torture,' said Margaret. 'When it's going on all you do is think how to endure it. It's when it stops and you think about it that you learn to dread it.'

She dreaded it less for herself than for her baby. John George was nearly four months old, old enough to start in alarm at unexpected noises. But although he sometimes cried when awakened in the night or whimpered when he sensed his mother's fear he was the least badly affected of any of them. He, at any rate, didn't spend the days in a haze of fatigue dreading what the night might bring.

Two days before Christmas Tony, smart in his sub-lieutenant's uniform, came home on leave. He arrived unexpectedly late in the evening and asked Jean if she could find him a bed.

'But what about your father?' she asked. 'Won't he be waiting for you?'

'He doesn't know I'm coming. It wasn't certain whether I'd get off and I didn't want to raise any false hopes. I'd rather not disturb him now. He always goes to bed early these days. Besides, it's been a difficult journey. I'm not sure I can face him tonight.'

Jean was in two minds about what to do. All her natural instinct for hospitality urged her to make room for Tony. But she felt a responsibility towards Sefton, too. It had been plain to her on Tony's last visit home that he and his father were getting on no better than they had ever done. Indeed there had been hardly any contact between them at all.

When Tony had worked for his father they had at least discussed business together and even if the discussions had been conducted on a level of barely concealed disagreement Jean thought that that was better than nothing. Better at least than the indifference that Tony had appeared to show towards his father since he had joined the Navy.

Jean wished that there was something she could do to reconcile the two of them, but there was not. Had she suggested to either of them that a reconciliation was necessary they would have denied it. They had had no outright quarrel, it was simply that the differences between them had grown wider over the years. Looking at Tony's tired face when he came in out of the dark night Jean was forced to admit that this was not the best moment to interfere.

'All right,' she said. 'You may as well have Philip's bed for the night. I'm afraid he won't be coming back for Christmas.'

In the event Tony never managed to get into bed at all. The siren went before he had finished his cocoa. Edwin, with a weary sigh, reached for his warden's hat and prepared to go out.

'Oh, Edwin,' Jean said. 'You look so tired. Must you go down to the post tonight?'

'Now, Jean, you know I must. It might be a heavy night and we're rather short down there since Peter ... Ted will be expecting me. Anyway, it'll be one less in the shelter. You'll have room to spread yourselves without me.'

'Shelter?' Freda was shrill and edgy. 'I'm not going in that shelter. I just won't, not tonight. I'd rather ... I can't bear it. It's damp and smelly and it ... frightens me. I'll stay in the house.'

'Now, Freda ...' Edwin was going to insist but Jean, with a gesture stopped him. She had lived with Freda's nervousness for a month now. She had a good idea of its cause.

'All right, then. You can go under the stairs. But not on your own, mind. Someone must ...'

'I will,' offered Tony. 'Under the stairs will be quite a home from home. I'm used to cramped quarters now. I'll look after her and Robert can look after you. It might only be for an hour.'

Freda and Tony made themselves as comfortable as they could, sitting up with their backs against the wall.

'You should try and get some sleep,' Tony said.

'No.' Freda shook her head. 'I don't feel like sleeping. I can't sleep through it. I used to be able to, but not just now.'

'It is pretty noisy.'

'It's not that. I just want to be awake. Ready ... How is it in the wavy Navy, then?'

'Oh, a bit boring, actually.'

'Yes, that's it. It's boring here, too. You should tell Robert that. Mum wants him putting off the idea of going to sea. The thought of all that cold water scares her.'

'That?' Tony laughed. 'That's what keeps the vessel afloat.'

'Oh, Tony!'

'Nice to see you smile.'

'Sorry. I know I'm not what Mum calls my usual self. But it gets you down.'

'I heard.'

'Mmm.'

'Anyway, Christmas soon. I gather your Aussie boy-friend's coming.'

'Yes. Mum invited him. Out of sympathy for him and a mistaken idea of what I need to buck me up.'

'Her idea's mistaken?'

'Yes.'

The noise of the raid had been building up around them, but apart from an occasional involuntary movement from Freda neither of them had taken any notice of it. Now the sound was much nearer and by unspoken consent they stopped talking to listen.

Suddenly there was a rattle and a clatter above their heads, a crashing thud and the house shook. Freda and Tony stared at each other, each waiting for the other to say what they dared not.

'Was that...?' asked Tony. Freda nodded and reached out to open the door. She was so convinced that it would not yield that when it did she fell head over heels into the hall.

'Are we hit?' asked Tony.

'No. I mean yes.' Freda was so relieved she shouted.

'What?'

'But it's only little. It's only upstairs. We're all right.' She sat on the floor smiling beatifically round the undamaged hall.

'Not so all right,' said Tony. 'Come on.' Already he could hear the crackle of flames and smell the smell of burning and, being less shocked then Freda, he had weighed up what must be done. 'It was an incendiary,' he said. 'Bring water, sand. Have you got a stirrup pump? Come on, Freda.'

Robert burst in through the front door.
'The roof,' he said. 'It's all on fire. And there's one in the garden but that's just in earth so Margaret can cope. Come on, or we'll be burnt down.'
Freda roused herself and reached for the phone. 'I'll get Dad,' she said. 'Take the blankets off my bed, they might smother it.' But Robert and Tony had already gone racing up the stairs.
When Edwin arrived breathless and fearful as a result of Freda's phone call they had everything under control. Robert was glorying in the excitement of it all, presenting himself as the hero of the hour.
'Good job I looked out of the shelter,' he said. 'We got there just in time with the eiderdown.'
'Not my eiderdown?' said Jean.
'No, Freda's. And Tony had the water of course . . .'
'It'll be ruined,' said Jean.
'It was either that or the house,' said Robert. 'We stopped it burning down.'
'Hold on a minute.' Margaret was rocking her baby. 'What about us in the garden? Me and the dustbin lid. That one could have spread, you know.'
'Well, well, how about some tea, Jean?' Edwin took off his tin helmet and mopped at his forehead. 'You've all managed very well. I thought I'd get here to find the whole house gone up in smoke from what Freda said.'
'I never said . . .' Freda was a little sensitive over the part she had played.
'And so it would have done,' said Edwin pacifically, 'if you hadn't all been so quick. I could do with you lot fire-watching at the works.'
'All's well that ends well,' said Jean, 'apart from the mopping up. We'll get a tarpaulin over the hole and get Sefton to find a builder. And then when it's mended we'll be as good as new. As if it had never happened.'
But the bomb was yet to do damage that was less easily mended than a hole in the roof.
The next morning, Christmas Eve, after Tony had been set on his way to make what he could of a reunion with his father, Jean set out with the family ration books and Robert as her porter to get in the last minute things for Christmas. Margaret

settled the baby and went up into the damp, charred boxroom to make what order she could out of the chaos that the bomb had made.

Flurries of sheet blew in through the jagged hole in the roof and made her shiver. It seemed strange and rather frightening to see this room that had always been so dark and cosy that it had seemed like a hidey hole in the heart of the house suddenly exposed to the outside light and air.

Margaret moved what she could to the more protected corners of the room and heaped the burned remains of Freda's pink eiderdown into an empty cardboard carton. She could see now quite clearly what had happened. The bomb had crashed straight through the tiles and rafters above her head and only the fact that it had landed directly on top of a sturdy tin chest of Jean's had stopped it crashing through the floor and wreaking further havoc down below.

The tin chest was battered but still intact. It had saved the house from destruction. Margaret tried to move it but it was too heavy for her so, with some difficulty, she lifted the distorted lid.

Inside, unharmed, were bundles of letters tied up with ribbon. Without really thinking what she was doing Margaret took one out and read it. It was a love letter, written on thick smooth paper that smelt sweetly of unburned tobacco. It was written to Jean. It was only when Margaret got to the end of it that she realised, with surprise, that it had not been written by her father.

Margaret put the letter back in the box and wondered what to do. She must somehow, she decided, let her mother know that the box had been revealed for all to see without admitting that she knew what was in it. The letter she had read had shed a new light on her mother. Jean once, she realised, had been an impetuous, self-willed girl. Was that girl still there, hidden by the practical woman that her mother had been compelled by circumstances to become?

When Margaret got downstairs the baby was crying. He had been awakened by the ringing of the doorbell. Margaret picked him up and went to the door.

Owen stood diffidently on the step.

'Er . . . hello,' he said in his Australian twang.

'Oh, come in,' said Margaret. 'You're early.'

'I'm sorry. I was just lucky with the trains. Shall I come back later?'

'No, of course not. You must come in. Freda's still at work, but she won't be long. She's on an early shift now. You're just in time. I was going to start the lunch. Put your thing's down and come into the kitchen.'

'I'm so sorry if it's an inconvenience . . .'

'It isn't. Don't worry. In fact, you can be positively useful. Hold the baby while I get on with the potatoes.'

Owen sat, ill at ease, watching Margaret.

'Are you sure there's nothing I can do?' he asked.

'You're doing fine.' Margaret said. 'Just hold John George until he drops off.'

'Drops off?'

Margaret laughed at the look on Owen's face.

'Goes to sleep, I mean,' she said.

'Oh, I see. And then I thought perhaps that if you know what time Freda comes out I might go and meet her.'

'Well . . .' Margaret wondered how much she ought to warn him about Freda's change of heart. 'I don't know about that.'

'Why not?'

Margaret pushed the tin opener into a tin of corned beef and looked at Owen.

'It's better you should know, I suppose. She's finding life a bit difficult at the moment. You know that Peter Collins was killed? Just after that . . . you know. Well, I don't want you to get the wrong idea. He meant nothing to her, really, not in the way of . . . love. But she had known him a long time and his mother . . . Freda was very upset by it. She feels responsible in some way, though really that bomb could have dropped anywhere. What I'm trying to say is that you might find her rather changed. Just give her time, that's the best thing.'

Owen's face was serious. 'Thank you,' he said. 'Thanks for telling me that. Freda's important to me.'

'Yes.' Margaret cut him short. She was so used by now after half a year without John, to controlling her own emotions that she disliked any display of emotion in other people. She hoped that Owen would keep his feelings for Freda on a tight rein. Otherwise, she thought, it was going to be a pretty difficult Christmas.

The rest of that day was hectic. All afternoon the house was filled with people: Robert hanging paper chains, Owen, trying to be inconspicuous, Jean and Freda wrapping parcels. Edwin came in early with two men from the works who had to fix a tarpaulin over the hole in the boxroom roof.

All the coming and going made the baby fractious. Margaret had promised her mother that she would do the Christmas baking. She counted up on her fingers. Even with Philip and David away and Sheila visiting her children, and not counting John George who was too small for mincepies, there would be eight for Christmas dinner. Margaret looked ruefully at the small jar of mincemeat that was all her mother had been able to get. If that was all there was it would just have to do. Margaret and Jean were getting good at making things do.

So it wasn't until teatime that Margaret remembered about the letters. Her father came downstairs with the workmen and showed them out through the front door. But then, instead of going, as he usually did at the end of each day, to give Jean a kiss and ask her what there was for tea he went straight away to the table and sat waiting for his meal.

Margaret went to have a word with her mother.

'Mum,' she said. 'Up in the boxroom ... I found your old tin chest this morning.'

'Did you?' Jean was busy at the stove.

'I don't know whether you want to move it. I don't know whether there might be anything ... private in it.'

'Oh.' Jean bit her lip. 'Thank you, Margaret. You didn't by any chance see a long, buff envelope in there, did you?'

'I don't know.' Margaret was ill at ease. 'I didn't know what was in it.'

In fact, though Margaret did not know it, it was not the letters that had upset Edwin. He had known all about them for years; they were only powerless sentimental relics of something that had been over for Jean long before he had met her. What Edwin had found in the box when he had been up in the attic supervising the workmen was something which had touched his pride far more deeply. Something Margaret would have dismissed without a second glance. It was a copy of Jean's father's will.

As he had read it by the light that filtered down through the gap in the roof Edwin had been furious. Because the will instructed that when her mother, that frail old lady in a Bournemouth nursing home, died, Jean would get a quarter of her father's estate. Edwin had always understood that this was not so. For years Jean had led him to believe that all she would ever inherit was a tiny fraction of her father's estate.

So Jean would be provided for. There had been no need, all these years, for Edwin to kowtow to Sefton for the sake of the pension that Sefton had at last so grudgingly offered him.

All Edwin's old resentment of Jean's family boiled up. He had, he thought, been tied to Sefton by a trick, and he was immensely hurt that Jean should apparently have connived at this. At any rate, he knew now, and it was not too late. At last he was free to do as he chose. He resolved that as soon as possible after Christmas he would act. He would go and see Dennis Pringle.

For as long as Margaret could remember Jean and Edwin had gone through an unvarying ritual on Christmas Eve. Sometime in the evening when the bulk of the preparations for the next day had been made, Edwin would settle Jean in the best armchair and put her feet up on the pouffe. Then he would bring her, with a flourish and a little speech about building her strength up for the next day, a tiny glass of sherry, and Jean would sip it and bask in his attention.

This evening there was the sherry, but there was no speech, no attention. Edwin filled the glass and gave it to Jean but he did so almost brusquely. Margaret noticed, and felt sad. She didn't like to see her parents at odds.

Sefton and Tony were, as usual, coming round for Christmas Dinner. The day would not have been complete for Jean without her brother but his company was less than a pleasure for the rest of the family. Edwin always felt uneasy when Sefton was in his house. As the host he should have been the master of ceremonies but with Sefton there he found it difficult to take the lead. Sefton's tart remarks reminded him perpetually who was really the boss, Sefton's appraising glances never let him forget who was really the owner of this house.

In fact Sefton was not quite his usual fiery self that Christmas. Tony had arrived at home to find his father far from well. He had quarrelled, not for the first time, with his housekeeper and then, just after she had left, gone down with the flu.

In spite of his distaste for his father Tony had been sorry to find him so weak and lonely. Sefton under full steam was someone to disagree with, to dislike, even to hate. But a Sefton humbled by illness, struggling to look after himself alone in that big empty house because his pride would not let him ask for help, was someone to pity. Tony had spent the best part of Christmas Eve putting the house to rights and making peace with the housekeeper.

The festive meal that year was not a success. Jean had been unwell all day and spent most of the morning in bed; Margaret, left on her own to do the cooking was overtired and irritable. Freda was ill at ease with Owen and he with her. Sefton, forgetting with his usual lack of tact, that Robert was due to join a ship in two days held forth over the pudding about the dangers of life at sea.

Only Robert and Tony were in anything like a holiday mood and eventually the general low spirits subdued them too. Nobody was sorry when the food was gone and the King's speech over and they were free to disperse. None of them felt like party games.

Sefton and Tony went home and Jean took her headache back to bed. Edwin tried to doze in his armchair but although his eyes were closed he did not sleep. These days it was not easy to find time to think and he had a lot to think about.

Late in the afternoon he went upstairs to see Jean. She was lying well to the side of the big bed even though she had it to herself. The previous evening Edwin had moved his things into Philip's empty bedroom. For the first time in thirty years he and Jean had slept apart.

The reason they had given for the change was that they slept more peacefully if they had a bed to themselves. This was partly true, but it was not the whole story. The separation marked a real rift: Jean could not forgive Edwin for signing Robert's papers and now he could not forgive her for, as he thought, deceiving him. As she lay, weak and small, in one corner of the bed, Edwin felt sorry that this was so. But he made no gesture of reconciliation. He had waited thirty years for the courage to break with Jean's family. He did not want to dissipate that courage by weakness now.

CHAPTER TEN

Dennis Pringle was the head of a family printing works slightly larger than Sefton's and a good deal more-go-ahead. The two firms had been competitors for a generation. Edwin had been slightly acquainted with Pringle for years—the world of printing was a small one—but the visit he was contemplating was not a social one. Edwin knew that Pringle had lost his manager to the army, and that the job was his for the asking.

None the less he told nobody where he was going when he set off to keep his appointment with Pringle. He could not get away from the feeling that he was doing something underhand. And yet, he told himself, he had a perfect right to offer his services freely on a free market. Any obligation that he owed to Sefton he had surely paid a hundredfold.

For years past he had carried responsibilities without due credit. Now at last the way was open for him to reap the rewards that Sefton had denied him.

Even so, as he walked the short distance between his own works and Pringle's Edwin was haunted by a sense of guilt. It wasn't the image of Jean that filled his mind, nor of Sefton; he was thinking of his father.

That fierce old man lived alone in such proud independence that he would not even visit his son in what he called 'yon big house of yourn' for a quite groundless fear of being patronised. He had said to his son the last time Edwin had gone to the home of his childhood: 'So you're a manager now.' The remark had been made with distrust as well as with pride. Edwin could not help feeling, as he knocked on Pringle's door, that he was doing something his father would never have done. Was he not, by paying Sefton in his own coin, becoming a little like Sefton himself?

Dennis Pringle received him cordially. He was a handsome, urbane man, about Sefton's age but a different kind of person altogether. Everything about him, and his office, and the works which Edwin had just walked through, had polish. The works were equipped with up-to-date machinery that Edwin could not help but envy. The old machines that Sefton had refused to replace just before the war were increasingly giving trouble with the demands that were now being put on them and with the supply situation getting tighter every day it was becoming more and more difficult to find spare parts to mend them with. Edwin marked it up in favour of Pringle that he was obviously both forward-looking and businesslike when it came to equipment.

'Well,' said Pringle, when the preliminary courtesies were over, 'has my man shown you round?'

'Yes, thank you.'

'And did you like what you saw?'

'Yes, very much. Some of those new flat-beds are the very latest design.'

'Got them in the nick of time, just before the war started. Can't get hold of them for love nor money now, everybody's gone over to munitions these days. So I suppose we're as up to date as anybody you'll find anywhere. It does help, you know, to be efficient. Helps us to pay good wages and ... er ... salaries. Substantially more than other people, in the case of management.'

Edwin made another mental note in Pringle's favour. The meeting, he thought, was going well. His feelings of unease were beginning to fade.

'How are you placed,' he asked, 'for personnel?'

'Not too badly, not too badly at all, I'm happy to say.' Pringle leaned back in his leather chair and the watch chain across his waistcoat shifted and gleamed. 'Of course we've had to let some of them go into the services, the younger ones, but I've still got most of the men who've been with me for years. Enough to manage with, anyway. Of course they've stayed with me because I know how to look after them. You have to know how to look after the men, wouldn't you agree?'

'Oh, very much.'

'I mean,' said Pringle, smoothing his shining hair, 'you have to accept responsibility for them. The working man has no sense of responsibility, how can he have when he hasn't been brought up to it? That's where we come in. We must accept responsibility for them.'

'Mmm,' said Edwin doubtfully.

Pringle leaned forward and pressed the bell on his desk. Then he put his hands out in front of him, fingertips together, one crossed thumb striking the other in a perpetual self-congratulatory caress that Edwin didn't like.

'Sefton, now,' Pringle went on, 'doesn't see it the same way, I'm sure. To him his workers should be ruled with a rod of iron. He doesn't see them, as I do, as children. Yes, that's right, children. I hadn't quite thought of putting it like that before, but it's a very apt comparison. Don't you think so, Mr Ashton? The carrot rather than the stick is my method.'

There was a discreet tap on the door and Dennis Pringle's secretary came in.

'Ah, Miss Burton. Mr Ashton, this is my indispensable Miss Burton. She's going to make us some tea, aren't you, my dear? The larger pot today, and two cups, please.'

Edwin found the atmosphere in the office oppressive. The gleaming uncluttered desk with its silver ornaments made him feel out of place. He noticed with embarrassment that he had a smear of oil on the back of his hand. He must have got that when he'd stopped on his way out to look at the machine that had been giving trouble all morning. Surreptitiously he rubbed it against his trouser leg.

'No thank you,' he said. 'No tea for me. I really haven't much time.'

'Oh,' said Pringle, 'but we must discuss . . .'

Warning bells rang in Edwin's mind. He must, he thought, at all costs avoid committing himself this afternoon. A change of the kind that he was contemplating couldn't be undertaken lightly. There were a lot of factors to take into consideration and Edwin was not at all sure that he could consider them dispassionately while he was within range of Pringle's smooth voice. He felt, suddenly, very very wary of Pringle.

'The fact is,' he said, 'that I have to be back to meet someone at half past. Of course our discussion has given me plenty of food for thought.'

'Of course,' said Pringle. 'I quite realise that you'll need time to think, time perhaps to discuss matters with . . . with your wife and family perhaps. So long as you're quite clear about how I stand.'

'Quite clear, thank you.'

'Bearing in mind of course that I shall be only too happy to discuss anything . . . salary perhaps . . . in greater detail if you want to.'

'Thank you,' said Edwin again. 'I'm sorry to rush off.'

'Don't mention it. I fully appreciate how busy a man in your position is. You'll be in touch then?'

'That's right. I'll be in touch.'

For four days Edwin brooded about what to do. He scratched old wounds, reminding himself of the slights Sefton had dealt him over the years, of the occasions when people had been promoted over his head or his advice had been disregarded. He remembered how Sefton had for so long made him feel the poor relation, the boy who had wormed his way in by marrying the boss's daughter. Against that he contrasted the position he would have at Pringle's. There he would be manager in his own right with no strings attached. He would be able to do what he wanted and he would have the equipment to do so efficiently. He would be his own man at last.

But although the right course of action seemed so obvious, still Edwin hesitated. He was held back from decision by some instinctive feeling that it would not be right, a feeling that he tried to dismiss on the grounds that it was no more than timidity, a natural reluctance to disturb a pattern of life that had been so long set.

It was, strangely enough, a letter from Philip, far away 'somewhere in Africa' and knowing nothing of the matter that showed him plainly the reason for his unease. Philip, writing circumspectly because of the censor, described one of his officers as 'just like Mr Pringle'.

Suddenly Edwin saw Pringle through Philip's eyes. Pringle, though he thought himself so enlightened, patronised his workers with all the arrogance of someone who was firmly convinced of his own superiority. If Edwin worked for Pringle he would have to do the same. There would be no more of the easy relationship of equals that he had with his men now. If he went to work for Pringle he would have to change sides, become a boss's man. If he did that he would have to repudiate all that his father had brought him up to believe.

At least so long as he was with Sefton he would have no need to do that. His relationship with Sefton did at least have the virtue of honesty. Both Sefton and he had no doubt about whose side he was on.

Edwin decided, after all, that he would stay where he was.

With his decision made Edwin felt much happier. He would have been willing now to make up his quarrel with Jean but as the time for Robert's departure drew near she blamed Edwin more and more for signing the papers. So Edwin soon gave up trying for reconciliation.

In a way he was relieved that he need not share his thoughts with Jean. A worry shared, people said, was a worry halved, but Edwin was not so sure of that. Perhaps, he thought, if he and Jean didn't talk about their fears for Robert, they would go away.

In his stronger moments Edwin knew that such an attitude was foolish. But he preferred to bury his head in the sand because he was, like so many other people, bone weary. He was weary of war, of sleepless nights, of self-denial and of anxiety, but he could see no end to any of these things.

The Ashtons spent New Year's Eve at home on their own. Freda had arranged to go to a dance but her date had been called off at the last moment; she was not in a good mood.

'There we are,' she said, reaching across to switch off the radio as the last of Big Ben's twelve strokes faded away, 'It's nineteen forty-one. Cheers, I suppose.' She drained the last drops of watery, saccharined cocoa from her mug. 'I'm off to bed.'

Upstairs Margaret's baby let out a thin wail. Margaret, deep in an armchair, looked at the ceiling towards the noise and sighed.

'There's somebody doesn't seem too pleased about the New Year,' she said.

'He's not the only one, is he?' asked Freda, staring at her father. The coldness between Edwin and Jean was obvious to their children and in Freda's eyes at least, Edwin was to blame. That morning Robert had set off to join a ship as an apprentice. Jean had packed his suitcase full with hand-knitted gloves and biscuits made with most of the rest of the family's sugar and fat rations for a week. She had seen him off with a smile on her face, but as soon as he was out of sight her tears had flowed. Freda, comforting her mother and crying too, herself, would not have listened even if Edwin had tried to explain that he no more wanted Robert to go to sea than she did but that he respected Robert's right to choose for himself. Besides, he knew, as Freda did not, that the fact that he had signed Robert's papers was by no means the whole cause of the trouble between himself and Jean. So he smiled conciliatingly at his youngest daughter and said: 'Happy New Year, love. Happy New Year, all of you. Let's hope . . .'

Jean came through from the hall where she had been taking a long distance phone call.

'Is it time?' she asked. 'Has it struck? Oh, well . . . let's hope for the best for us all. That was the matron of Mother's nursing home on the phone.'

'At this time of night?' asked Margaret. 'Is it something serious?'

'She's been taken into hospital, and at her age . . . I said I'd go down there tomorrow.'

'To Bournemouth?' Freda was appalled. 'It'll take hours. Tony said the trains were terrible when he came up for Christmas. He had to stand in the corridor nearly all the way.'

'I must go.' Jean put a hand up and rubbed her eyes that still ached from weeping for Robert. 'Matron thought I should. I feel rather bad really about her being so far away, anyway, but the specialist did recommend this place so highly.'

'You'd better get to bed straight away, then,' said Edwin. 'Get what sleep you can. I'll look up a train. We could all do with getting to bed.'

Sheila got up from her chair over by the table. She had been so quiet that they had almost forgotten that she was there.

'I'd better be off,' she said. 'I don't think David'll phone now, do you?' She looked thinner than ever, and on her pale face the lines of worry had etched deeper since her children had gone away. Edwin remembered the pretty, happy girl she had been when she had first come to his house and, not for the first time, felt angry at what his son had done to her.

'You can't walk home now,' he said. 'You must stay the night. David might still get through. I daresay he's tried and the line was busy. Perhaps he'll try again.'

They were all silent, contemplating David's dereliction. Sheila had been waiting since nine o'clock for the phone call that had not come.

'I'm sure he will have tried,' said Jean without conviction. 'You must stay.'

'I'll make the bed up.' Margaret was brisk. 'Mum, you must get to bed if you've got a journey. And Freda's got to go to work tomorrow. Off you go, all of you. Sheila and I will cope. She can bed down on the settee, then she's near the phone. All right, Sheila?'

When the others had gone Sheila said: 'Is the baby good?'

'Can't complain.' Margaret plumped up a pillow. 'He's settled down to a routine so I'm leaving him to Mum after the holidays and going back to teach. Did you know?'

'No, but I'm sure that's best. You don't want to have too much time to brood.'

'Mmm.' Margaret gave Sheila a sharp glance. 'Janet and Peter all right?'

'Oh yes, they're all right. They like it in the country and the lady's very good to them. Like a mother ... they'll think of her like a mother by the time it's finished.'

'Oh no.' Margaret was moved by the tremor in Sheila's voice to put a hand on her shoulder. 'They won't do that. They're old enough to understand why they've had to go away. So long as you go and see them and write and so on. They'll be all right.'

Margaret could feel Sheila's shoulders shaking. She was tired, and above her head she could hear her son starting to cry again, this time in a way that she knew would not diminish but build up to a crescendo. She had not bargained for becoming Sheila's confidante but she could not back out now.

'And then there's David.' Sheila was sobbing openly now, 'He hardly ever writes and when he says he'll phone, he doesn't ... I'm sure he won't now. What's happening to him? What's he up to? I don't know what will become of us.'

'Now, now.' Margaret found that she was patting Sheila's back with the same gestures that she used to wind John George. 'David never was a great letter-writer, was he? He hasn't got the knack. He always finds it so much easier to talk to people when he's actually with them.'

She tried to shut out the sound of the baby's yells and thought about what she had just said. On reflection it didn't seem very helpful. Suddenly she had an idea. 'I know what would be best,' she said. 'Couldn't you get some time off from the canteen? I'm sure you must be due for some. Then you could go and see him and you'd know that everything was all right.'

So it was that three days later Sheila packed her suitcase and set off to see David. She didn't write to tell him she was going. She had written him three letters in succession without anything more than a brief postcard in reply and pride made her refuse to write any more.

Margaret's suggestion that she should go to see David had seemed to her to be a revelation. For months now she had been lonely and worried. When she saw David occasionally for a few brief days when he came home on leave everything seemed all right but as soon as he had gone again her anxieties came back.

Sheila knew David well enough to know his weaknesses. She did not doubt that when he told her he cared for her and the children he meant what he said at the time, but, with David, out of sight was out of mind. It suddenly seemed to her that if she could see him at the base, meet his friends and let them know her, everything would be all right. She would re-establish herself in David's eyes and in theirs as his wife. Then she would be safe. After going down there she would have no more need to worry.

Sheila had timed her visit well. How well, she was never to know. She only knew that she was pleased at the warmth of her reception when, having enquired at the Air Base and been directed, to her surprise, to the W.V.S. study centre she eventually met up with David.

Once his first astonishment at seeing her was over he clung to her with a fervour greater than she remembered for a long time. She hadn't known, she thought, how much he'd missed her. She hadn't known how much he'd needed her. She couldn't know that she had turned up just at the moment when his bruised self-esteem most needed the balm of her admiration, because luckily for her, she didn't know how he had felt about Susan Reynolds.

Susan ran the study centre. She, not a thirst for learning, was the reason why David spent so much of his time there. She was the widow of one of David's old crew mates and as such had been glad of his friendship. But to David friendship had not been enough.

He had fallen, more deeply than at first he had realised, under Susan's spell. The difference between them did not matter to him. He did not care that Susan was more educated than he was, that what interested her was books and music and art, all the things that David had no time for. To David the attraction that she held for him was enough. He would not recognise that the attraction was not mutual.

Susan liked David well enough. He had been her husband's friend and his company saved her from loneliness. Besides, David was a nice-looking man and she had been flattered by his attention. But further than that she was not willing to go.

The whole thing had come to a head at last. David's pursuit of Susan had grown fiercer over many months. She had tried her best to discourage him but he had been impervious to all her hints and all her excuses. Finally, on the morning of the day that Sheila arrived, Susan had confronted David with the truth. She had told him bluntly that she did not nor could not be other than a friend to him.

Sheila, revelling in David's ardour, did not know herself a substitute. She was simply glad that he needed her.

'Well, well,' she said to him, stroking his hair as they lay on her bed in the hotel bedroom, 'they say that absence makes the heart grow fonder. Are you glad I came?'

'What do you think?'

'I would have come before, if you'd asked me.'

'Yes. Well . . . I thought you were busy at that canteen.'

'I am. But we're allowed a bit of time off, even in war-time. Shall I come again?'

'Yes, yes, if you want. Only let me know . . .'

'You know those notices? The ones that say "Is your journey really necessary! ?" I think mine was, don't you?'

'You can say that again,' said David.

CHAPTER ELEVEN

Once Edwin had made up his mind that he would not go to work for Pringle he put the matter out of his mind. He would have been horrified if he had known that Sefton had a good idea of what had been going on. Sefton and Pringle belonged to the same club and once he realised that Edwin was not after all going to accept his offer Pringle saw no reason for discretion.

Sefton grasped the implications at once. If Edwin had been willing to make a move for the first time in thirty years he might be willing to do so again. The old order of things was changing. Sefton, bolstered though he was against the rigours of war with his contacts, his black market whisky and his share in a backyard pig, could see that things would not always be so comfortable for men like him. The war was stirring things up, giving people a taste for independence. He realised that his old subtle ascendency over Edwin was broken.

And in time Sefton's position would become weaker. When his mother died, as it seemed she soon would, her shares in the firm would be distributed. Sefton himself would get only thirty per cent of them. The rest would be distributed between Tony, Jean and the other sister, Helen, who lived in London.

Sefton did his sums. Edwin would have effective control of Jean's shares and would be certain to stand with Tony against him. Helen, the younger sister, would align herself with Jean, if only to pay off old grudges. She and Sefton had never got on even as small children. So when it came to a crunch, and Sefton could see only too clearly that it might, Sefton would lose control of the business that he had dominated for years. To a man of Sefton's temperament such a prospect was intolerable, and he wracked his brains to find a way round the problem.

It was, ironically enough, Tony who all unwittingly, pointed the way to a solution. When Tony came home for a week's leave some time in the early spring he noticed a change in his father, a softening.

In fact, Sefton was lonely without Tony. He did, though he was incapable of showing it, love his son and when Tony was at sea he was afraid for him. Besides, it was lonely in the big house with only the housekeeper for company. So when he had Tony at home Sefton put himself out to please him.

Tony took advantage of his father's mood to put in a word for Edwin. Sefton was talking about the difficulties of maintaining all his property while both men and materials were in short supply.

'I can think of someone who wouldn't mind having a problem like that?' Tony said.

'Can you?' asked Sefton. 'Who's that?'

'Uncle Edwin.'

'Edwin? Why bring him into it?' Sefton was wary. 'What exactly are you driving at, Tony?'

'I'm only saying, in a roundabout kind of way, that I've been having a talk with him, and I think he would like to own the roof over his head.'

Sefton was genuinely surprised. 'Would he? Do you mean he wants to own that house? But he's had it rent free all these years.'

'It's not quite the same, is it?' Tony said.

'A damn sight better, if you ask me.'

'But it's tied to the job, Father. It makes him feel chained. Or is that the idea?'

'Must you talk in riddles, Tony.' Sefton was impatient. 'How am I supposed to know what you mean.'

'I think you do, Father,' Tony said. 'Has Uncle Edwin worked for you all these years because it was in his own best interests, do you think? Or because he had no choice unless he wanted to see his family out on the street. Times are changing, Father. Those kind of chains aren't going to last much longer.'

'What are you trying to say? That I should offer to let Edwin buy the house? Where would he get the money from?'

'A mortgage, perhaps.'

'At his age?' said Sefton. 'Don't be more foolish than you can help, Tony.'

'Well, then.' Tony's calm had been eroded by his father's provocation. 'Make him a present of it.'

'A present?'

'A share in the pig, Father. An interest in the business. Goodwill. There's more to management than money, Father, whether you see it or not.'

'Riddles again,' said Sefton. 'Anybody can tell you've no head for business, Tony. Soft, like your mother. God knows where you'd be if it wasn't for me.'

Later while he was tossing and turning in bed unable to sleep, Sefton thought again of what Tony had said. He had to admit that Tony was right. Whereas before all he had needed was Edwin's obedience, soon he would also need his goodwill. Giving Edwin the house he lived in would certainly obtain that.

But Sefton did not want to do it. To give something as solid and sure as a house in return for something as vague as goodwill, something that could not be measured or put down on a balance sheet, was not Sefton's style.

Then, suddenly, he thought what he would do. Sefton was so pleased with his plan that he put the light on and sat up in bed in his shrouded room while he examined it from every angle. The more he thought about it the better it seemed. With one gesture he had found a way to satisfy Tony, please Jean, and gain the ascendancy over Edwin.

He went over to see Jean as soon as he had finished breakfast the next morning. She was doing the washing when he arrived, rubbing the clothes on a board at the sink, but she was, as always, pleased to see her brother.

'Just let me put some things to soak,' she said, 'and then we'll go and sit down. This is a nice surprise, Sefton. You don't come often enough.'

'I come when I can, Jean. I'm a busy man, you should know that. But I thought you'd like to hear how I found Mother last week. I had a dreadful journey down there. The train was packed.'

'I know.' Jean was sympathetic. 'They always are. How was she, then?'

'She doesn't get any better. She hardly knew me.'

'But she does have better days? The matron told me she can be quite bright sometimes.'

'Not often.' Sefton was gloomy. 'She's not the woman she used to be, not by a long chalk, and won't be again. Do you remember how she used to play the piano for us?'

'And we'd sing? Those were happy days, Sefton.'

'I don't like to see her so changed.'

'We must all change, Sefton,' said Jean. 'We all grow old eventually.'

'Yes, I suppose so. Better not think about that too much, eh? I didn't come to make you miserable, Jean, I came to cheer you up. I've brought good news.'

'Have you?' Jean said. 'That'll be a nice change. What sort of news?'

'Well.' Sefton puffed out his chest. He felt genuinely pleased with himself. He had almost forgotten the ulterior motive behind the gesture he was about to make and was seeing it as pure altruism. 'Well, Jean, I'm offering to let you have the house.'

'The house?' Jean was astonished. 'This house? Buy it, do you mean? That's very kind, but where would we get the money from?'

'Yes. Well.' Sefton cleared his throat. He was coming to the tricky bit. 'I've thought about that. A mortgage would be out of the question, I realise that. You don't want a mortgage round your necks at your age. So I've thought of something else. Something that means the house will be yours without you finding any money, but there'll be no feeling of ... charity about it. All it needs is a gentleman's agreement between you and me.'

'Wait a minute, Sefton.' Jean felt that she was going out of her depth. 'This is very generous of you. I really am grateful and so will Edwin be. But don't you think you should come round when he's at home? He's the person who would understand all the business side of it, not me.'

'No, Jean.' To see Edwin was the last thing Sefton wanted. 'I never know when I shall find him in, these days. What with his fire-watching and his wardening, he's not at home that much, is he? Besides, it's you I'm doing it for really. You're my sister. I haven't forgotten the past you know, Jean. After all's said and done, blood's thicker than water.'

'But you know I don't like dealing with business matters, Sefton.'

'Don't worry your head about it. There's nothing to deal with. It's all quite simple. All it is ... I'm offering you the place, Jean, in return for the equivalent in shares in the business at current valuation. That's all.'

Jean looked puzzled. 'What shares?' she asked.

'Your shares, Jean. The ones you'll get when Mother dies. They're worth nothing now really, but I'm prepared to take them. Just so that you'll be able to feel that it's a proper transaction and the house is really yours.'

'Is that ... all right? Can I do that with the shares?'

'It'll be a "gentleman's agreement",' said Sefton. 'Just between you and me. There'll be no problem, we're just keeping things in the family, you see. It couldn't be simpler.'

Jean was still not reassured. For years now she had left all decisions except domestic ones to her husband. The very thought of dealing with money matters made her head spin.

'You'd do much better to talk about it with Edwin,' she said.

'Ah, but that's the point.' Sefton became conspiratorial. 'I know it sounds silly, but I don't want Edwin to know about the shares. It's a matter of pride. You know Edwin as well as I do.

Well, better, of course. Do you think he'd like it if he knew that you were buying the house for him? Because I don't. He's always been rather sensitive about Father's money, hasn't he? I think it would be better if he thought I was making him a present of it. A reward for past services you might call it. That's what I would like to do really, make it an outright gift, but with times being what they are . . . it's not easy, you know, for those of us with business responsibilities to keep our heads above water at a time like this. Let Edwin just look on it as a friendly gesture, eh? You've always wanted the two of us to be friends, haven't you?'

Jean was bemused by Sefton's flow of words. It was when he was in full flood like that with his fingers stuck into his waistcoat pockets that Sefton reminded her most vividly of her father. It wasn't a memory she relished. She wanted to quieten Sefton down.

'All right,' she said. 'I'll do just as you say. I suppose you know best.'

'That's right.' Sefton was beaming with satisfaction. 'Just tell Edwin it's a gift. I don't want any thanks. So long as I know you're happy, Jean, it's worth it to me.'

Under normal circumstances Jean might still, in spite of Sefton's words, have told Edwin about the bargain she had made with her brother, but because she still felt cool towards him she did not. She did not think it very important, anyway. She was no businesswoman. To her, shares simply represented money. She did not, as Sefton had, add thirty and twenty-five together, and make of them a majority vote. She had no idea that by agreeing to the exchange she had deprived Edwin of the chance of ever being his own master.

Edwin, thinking that the house was an outright gift, was at first incredulous and then delighted.

'It's ours?' he said to Jean. 'Are you sure? Why should he do such a thing?'

'I always said you misjudged Sefton. I've never understood why you could see no good in him. His bark's worse than his bite, that's all.'

'It looks as if you were right.' Pleasure made Edwin magnanimous. 'I almost feel I owe him an apology. This is our house now. I can hardly believe it, it seems too good to be true. It makes a difference to a man, you know, to live under his own roof.'

'You're pleased, then? I did the right thing . . . saying yes?'

'Pleased?' Edwin paused to search for the right word. 'I'm thrilled. I'm genuinely grateful to Sefton, and I shall certainly tell him so. It makes up for a lot, doesn't it, getting the house? It restores my faith in human nature. Sefton's made me a happy man today. I shall always be grateful to him for that.'

CHAPTER TWELVE

When the new term had started after Christmas Margaret had started teaching again, leaving her baby in Jean's care. The headmistress of her old school had welcomed her back with open arms. In spite of the air raids some of the children who had been evacuated had come back to Liverpool and at the same time all the younger male members of staff had gone into the army so Margaret's help was needed.

She was glad to be working again. She had not altogether enjoyed being at home with her mother all day. With Philip and Robert away there was not enough work about the house to occupy two women and once John George had settled into a steady routine of eating and sleeping, Margaret had found that the days dragged. She had had too much time to think.

In going back to work Margaret was trying to make a fresh start. She had finally abandoned all hope of ever seeing John again. The Porters had left Liverpool just before Christmas: Harry had found himself work in the country for the sake of Celia's precarious health. Margaret had helped them with the removal. As each piece of furniture had been carried out of the house that had been her only married home she felt that a chapter of her life was coming to a close. At the end of the day she had stood in the empty house shaking hands with Harry Porter and said a mental farewell to John.

It was not too difficult for her to get back into the old routine at school. She already knew many of the staff and easily remembered most of the children. One child in particular, Barbara Armstrong, she recollected with particular poignancy. Barbara's mother had died during the summer just before the war, about the time that Margaret had got married.

Margaret, like the rest of the staff, had known about it at the time and felt compassion for the girl. However, she had not known Barbara very well and had in any case been preoccupied with her own happiness so she had thought no more about it.

But now that she had Barbara in her class and it was obvious that the girl still felt her bereavement Margaret had especial sympathy for her. When the girl was difficult she tried to be patient and she took an extra interest in her work.

Barbara's father was a musician and therefore often free during the day. He frequently met Barbara outside school and often when Margaret saw him she would stop and talk over anything that bothered her about Barbara. Margaret enjoyed these little talks and began to prolong them. It surprised her to realise how much she must have missed the company of a young, attractive man.

Michael Armstrong must have enjoyed the talks too because he waited outside school with increasing frequency, and seemed as anxious to catch Margaret's eye as Barbara's. So it came as no great surprise when eventually, with some diffidence and hesitation, he asked Margaret to go to a concert with him.

She was glad to accept and soon she and Michael fell into a pleasant routine. One evening every week they would go to a concert or the pictures together. Then on Saturdays or Sundays they would walk with Barbara and John George in the wintry park or go for an occasional trip across the river.

Margaret never told her mother who she was going with when she set off on these expeditions. Indeed, without ever lying outright she let her mother believe she was going with a woman colleague from school. Her reticence was characteristic of her.

Of all the Ashton children Margaret had always been the one who kept her own counsel and this tendency had been increased by circumstances. Living as she was under her parents' roof it was difficult for her to prevent her mother treating her as if she were still a child. And yet it was important for Margaret to be established as a married woman in her own right. To do otherwise would be to deny John. And so Margaret had withdrawn into herself more than ever, keeping her life and her thoughts hidden from Jean.

The family however, without knowing the reason for it, noticed that Margaret was happier. Had they been able to see her when she was out with Michael they would have seen her happier still. On those outings Margaret managed to forget for a while her situation and enjoy herself without any thought for either the future or the past. For a few hours each week she became a girl again.

On their expeditions as a family group only Barbara was not happy. As she saw her father solaced by Margaret, Barbara grew more and more resentful. She made a fuss of John George but ignored his mother to an extent that Margaret could not help but notice.

However Margaret did not let this bother her. She thought that since she and Michael were no more than companions what his daughter thought was not very important. Margaret was convinced that Michael could never be more than a friend to her. Because he would never be a substitute for John nor she a substitute for his dead wife she did not expect that Michael might come to love her in her own right. She was quite unprepared therefore for what happened.

One cold night at the end of winter she and Michael went back to his house after a concert to have a cup of tea. This too had become part of their routine. On this particular night because the weather was wild the little house seemed especially cosy and welcoming. Margaret was not feeling at her best. The music had moved her deeply and to come out of the concert hall exhilarated only to have to face the realities of war, the blackout, the shortages and her own bereavement seemed unbearable. She turned to Michael for the comfort that he always so freely gave.

He listened while she told him how she felt.

'Oh, Margaret,' he said. 'I would do anything I could to make it better for you.'

'Thank you. I know you would.' Margaret felt ashamed of her self pity. Michael, too, was lonely.

'I'm sorry to go on about it,' she said. 'I suppose we are two of a kind. Cripples propping each other up.'

'Is that all you think it is?' Michael asked. 'I see you as more than just a stick to lean on.'

'I didn't mean it like that,' said Margaret. 'Of course you're more than that. I suppose my trouble is that when I'm happy

. . . and I can be happy when I'm with you . . . I have to look for the snags in it. Perhaps it's so as to be ready in case I lose the happiness again.'

'What you need is courage.' Michael was sitting very close to Margaret. He put his hand out to cover hers and his touch asked more than friendship.

Margaret kept her face averted but she did not move her hand from under his.

'Michael,' she said, 'I . . .' She didn't want to hurt him or reject him but thought somehow that she ought. Suddenly she was in a new situation when she had not had time to extricate herself from the old one. 'It's too soon,' she said. 'We're still tied up in other people.'

Michael put his free hand up to her face and turned her round to face him.

'No,' he said. 'We might think we are but they . . . those other people . . . are dead. We're not.'

'It's too soon.'

'Better too soon than too late,' Michael said, and started to kiss her.

Margaret could feel the warmth of his body. It was as comforting and as reassuring as a fire on a cold night. And she wanted to stay near it. She felt that she had no will of her own. She had stood on her own feet for so long now, being brave and sensible and level-headed, that she felt exhausted with the effort. She wanted somebody else to relieve her of the burden of any more decisions. She wanted Michael to take over her life, to decide for her what she should do. She leaned her weight on his shoulder and gave herself over to his lead.

Perhaps neither of them expected to go as far as they did, but neither of them took it upon themselves to call a halt. It was so sweet to be loved after long months of loneliness. Margaret was happy in Michael's arms, happy to please him and happy to be wanted.

It was afterwards that guilt came, after Michael had walked her home and kissed her good night very gently at the gate. Margaret let herself into the house, quietly because it was late, and ran upstairs quickly so as not to see anyone. Then, in the silence of her own room, she thought over what she had done and bitterly regretted it.

She felt that she had betrayed John. Her husband was less

than a year dead and she had been unfaithful to him. She forgot then all the mitigating circumstances, the combination of grief and need and affection and gratitude that had taken her into Michael's arms, the fact that the monotonous grind of daily life made harder than ever by war is sometimes the most difficult thing of all to endure. She remembered only the stark fact: John had gone to his death loving only her and she had not been able to endure more than a few months without him.

She had to punish herself, and she did so by refusing to see Michael again. For six weeks she inflicted on herself the life of a hermit, doing nothing but work or attend to her child. And she lived with the gradually increasing suspicion that her punishment was to be worse than that.

When she was sure beyond any doubt that she was pregnant Margaret was in despair. She could not confide in her family. One of the worst of her fears was the dread of what her mother and father would say.

She should have spoken to Michael but pride prevented her. In any case she did not see how telling him would help. She knew that if he knew of the position she was in he would want to marry her. He was an honourable man and he had said that he loved her. But Margaret was not free to marry. Because John's army tag had not been found and he was therefore still only posted missing Margaret was not legally a widow. She must wait seven years before she would be free to marry again. Telling Michael would make no difference to that.

The distress that Margaret was feeling communicated itself to her child. John George became fractious and miserable so that Margaret could not rest. At last, at breaking point, she poured out the whole story to Freda.

Freda, being detached, was able to be practical.

'You must tell Mum and Dad,' she said. 'And you must tell this Michael too. They'll find out some time, won't they? You'll have to tell them, Margaret.'

'I can't, I can't.' Margaret held her head and moaned. 'I can't face what they'll think. I feel so ashamed. I've let everybody down. I loved John, I really did. I do love him still. And this will kill Mum.'

'Mum's tougher than you think,' said Freda. 'She'll have to understand, and if she doesn't she'll have to learn to. Don't blame yourself so much, Margaret. This isn't really your fault.

It would never have happened if things had been normal. It's the war that's messed up your life, by taking John away. You'll not be the only one this kind of thing happens to, Margaret.'

'I'd feel better if you blamed me,' Margaret said. 'I do blame myself whatever you say. I can't see any way out of it, Freda. I just don't know what to do.'

'You must tell Mum and Dad.' Freda was definite. 'I'll tell them, if you don't. That's the first thing, Margaret. Once people know they'll accept it, they'll have to. Then ... perhaps you could get married.'

'You know I can't.'

'Why can't you?'

'For seven years. Because they're not sure about John.'

'Oh.' Freda was silent for a moment. 'Yes, I had forgotten that. You'll have to ... I don't know. We'll cross that bridge when we come to it. Now go upstairs. Just leave it to me. I'll break it to Mum and Dad.'

Margaret was only too glad to leave it to Freda. She was astonished to find how much Freda, who she had always thought of as her little sister, a rather feather-headed child, had hardened and toughened in the last two years. She was thankful that she had. Freda now seemed to be her only prop. Margaret could not have looked at her mother's face when she heard the news. She could hardly bear even to imagine how her mother would react.

Margaret listened through her bedroom door as Freda telephoned her father. Then she heard the front door click as her mother came back from a first-aid meeting and went into the living-room where Freda was waiting. Shame and despair engulfed her. Could she learn Freda's lesson and grow a tougher skin? Margaret reached for her coat and, creeping like a thief so that she would not be heard, let herself out of the house.

Jean took the news every bit as badly as Margaret had feared she would. She stared in disbelief at Freda as she stammered out the story and then, when she was finally convinced that it was true, railed against Margaret in shock and shame.

'How could she? How could she? I would never have thought it of Margaret behaving like a ... Why did she have to do it? We've done our very best for her. I don't know how I shall hold my head up.'

Edwin was calmer. 'What we did for Margaret wasn't enough for her,' he said. 'It wasn't our fault or hers, but how could we give her what she needed? We should have thought of that, not been so sure that she would get used to living on her own. She's only young, Jean.'

'But Margaret. She's the last one I would have thought ... What are we to do? What can she do?'

'That's her problem, isn't it?' Edwin said. 'She'll have to decide, she and ... the man. Perhaps if we'd let her stand on her own feet a bit more, not decided so much how she ought to behave, this wouldn't have happened. I'm going to bring her down now, Jean, and I want you to be kind to her. Tell her that you understand how it is with her. Whether you do or not, just tell her that you understand.'

But when Edwin came downstairs again it was without Margaret.

'She's not there,' he said, 'and her coat's gone. Did she say she might go out?'

'No,' said Freda. 'She just went up to be out of the way while I told you about it all. She was pretty desperate ...'

'Where can she have gone?' Edwin was anxious. 'She shouldn't have gone out. Do you know where she might be, Freda?'

'No, I don't. I know the name of the man, that's all. Someone at work is a neighbour of his. But I don't know his address.'

'If you know his name that'll do.' Edwin looked round for his hat. 'If he's in our sector Ted Fiddler will have him on the list at the Warden's Post. I'll go down there and see. It's worth a try.'

'Edwin.' Jean spoke for the first time since her outburst against Margaret. 'Edwin, don't tell Ted why you want to know.'

When he came out of the Warden's post Edwin was very angry. Even his anxiety for Margaret was overlaid by anger. Because Ted Fiddler's list had shown that as well as Michael Armstrong and his daughter there was a Mrs Janet Armstrong, Michael's wife, resident at eighteen Russel Street.

As he walked along through the black streets Edwin worked out what he would say to Armstrong. He was sure that Margaret must have been deceived. She would never knowingly have gone out with a married man. And what sort of a man could this Armstrong be, Edwin wondered, if he would deceive a person like Margaret.

Margaret was at Michael's house before him. Edwin smiled at her but he could not meet her eyes and he was glad when the child upstairs called for her. He wanted to talk to Armstrong alone.

Edwin was a peaceable man. He hated unpleasantness. But he was willing to face it in defence of his daughter.

'I suppose Margaret has told you about the position she's in,' he began.

'Yes, she told me just now.' Michael had the grace to look embarrassed. 'I can't say how sorry I am.'

Edwin tried to be calm. 'And have you told her your position, too?' he said.

'I've told her that I love her, and that there's nothing I'd like better than to marry her if I could.'

'If you could!' Edwin's voice was tight with contempt. 'Only you can't, can you? How dare you do this to my daughter.'

Michael faced Edwin bravely. 'Mr Ashton, I've said I'm sorry. I didn't mean this to happen. We were two lonely people...'

'What about your wife?' Edwin could not hold the accusation back any longer. 'Does Margaret know about her? I do, you see. I know that she's on the list as living here. We have records at the warden's post. We have you all grouped and classified. You can't deceive me, Mr Armstrong, even if you've deceived Margaret.'

'I have not deceived Margaret.' Michael was stung to indignation. 'That's the last thing I would do. My wife is dead.'

In spite of himself Edwin was impressed by the young man's straight gaze. He wanted to believe him.

'But our records,' he said. 'We've got her down.'

'Oh that. I can explain that.' Michael's indignation faded as rapidly as it had come. 'When the warden called my wife had just died. The month before in fact. She'd been in hospital...' Michael paused and looked up. Barbara's voice could be heard quite clearly from the bedroom above his head. 'I hadn't been able to tell my daughter ... cowardly, I suppose, but I was waiting for an opportunity. Barbara was with me when the man called.' Michael spread his hands wide and looked appealingly at Edwin. 'I just couldn't say it, not in front of her. The records didn't seem to matter. Do you understand?'

'I see.' Edwin was silent, thinking about the motherless child. From above their heads Margaret's voice could be heard now. She was singing to Barbara.

'I have a daughter too,' Edwin said. 'What about her?' He was no longer angry with Michael, just sorry for him and for Margaret.

Michael looked straight at Edwin. 'There's only one thing seems possible,' he said. 'I want to ask Margaret if she'll live here with me.'

Margaret and Edwin walked home together in silence. They both had a great deal to think about. Margaret had asked Michael for time to make her mind up. She didn't know what she should do. There were so many people she had to consider; her parents, the Porters and, above all, John George.

Edwin was relieved when Margaret did not ask his advice. He would not, for once, have known what to say to her. This was not the kind of situation that Edwin had ever expected to have to face.

Edwin felt very tired. Two years of war had knocked away from him some of the certainties of a lifetime. He was getting, he thought, too old to endure much more of it. Then he remembered Churchill. Churchill, after all, was older still and he could endure.

The night was quiet. The siren had gone but no raiders had come over. Edwin opened the front door for Margaret.

'Get a good night's sleep,' he said. 'Things might seem better in the morning.'